Larkin Dunton

A Memorial of the Life and Services of John D. Philbrick

Larkin Dunton

A Memorial of the Life and Services of John D. Philbrick

ISBN/EAN: 9783337400330

Printed in Europe, USA, Canada, Australia, Japan

Cover: Foto ©Andreas Hilbeck / pixelio.de

More available books at **www.hansebooks.com**

A

MEMORIAL

OF THE

LIFE AND SERVICES

OF

JOHN D. PHILBRICK

EDITED BY

LARKIN DUNTON, LL. D.
HEAD MASTER OF THE BOSTON NORMAL SCHOOL

BOSTON
NEW ENGLAND PUBLISHING COMPANY
1887

TO Mrs. Julia A. Philbrick, —

Whose wifely devotion and wise counsel comforted and strengthened her honored husband, and whose kindly and intelligent interest in education won the hearts of teachers, this volume is respectfully dedicated by

THE EDITOR.

"BE ASHAMED TO DIE WITHOUT HAVING ACCOM-
PLISHED SOME VICTORY FOR HUMANITY."

—*Horace Mann.*

PREFACE.

THIS volume is intended to be what its title implies, — a memorial of the life and services of him whom it commemorates. It is not meant to be in any sense a biography. Soon after the death of Dr. Philbrick, the desire was often manifested that the expressions of honor and esteem which had been called out on the occasion should be put into some form for permanent preservation. The death of no other educational man in this country has produced so profound and general a sense of personal loss ; for no other has been so well and so favorably known, and no other has left so strong an impress upon his age. It was not till he had been called to his reward, that the deep respect in which he was held, and the feelings of warm personal friendship with which he was regarded, found full expression.

Then, naturally, his more intimate friends wished to have the evidence of the love and honor which he had won preserved to the world. The present volume is an attempt to gratify that desire. It contains the addresses delivered at a public meeting held in Boston in his honor, a single paper from the pen of Dr. Philbrick himself, an account of his last sickness and death, the addresses at his funeral and at his final interment, some of the eulogistic letters written to the public press on the occasion of his death, the tributes paid to his memory by the Boston Masters' Association, the Schoolmasters' Club, and the School Committee of Boston, an account of the public memorial meeting in Boston, a letter from the Japanese minister to the United States, and resolutions adopted by various associations to which he was favorably known.

The addresses at the Boston meeting include an account of Dr. Philbrick's early life and education, by his friend, Gilman H. Tucker, of New York ; an account of his educational work in Boston, by the editor, and an estimate of his services to the cause of education in general by Dr. William T. Harris. From these addresses alone a stranger would be able to form a correct opinion of the man.

The paper selected to represent Dr. Philbrick himself is his address before the American Institute of Instruction, July, 1884, entitled, " Reform of Tenure of Office of Teachers." This was a subject in which he had long taken a deep interest, and it was this address that did much to secure favorable action upon the subject by the legislature of Massachusetts in 1886.

The papers and addresses contained in the volume constitute an honorable memorial to a noble man. If they assist in extending and perpetuating his memory, the editor's labor of love in preparing them for the press will be amply rewarded.

Boston, August, 1887.

CONTENTS.

———

Eulogistic Letters :

Early Life and Education

of

JOHN DUDLEY PHILBRICK.

———•——

By Gilman H. Tucker.

Early Life and Education

OF

JOHN DUDLEY PHILBRICK.

—————·—·—————

BIRTH, PARENTAGE, AND ANCESTRY.

The "Early Life and Education" of John Dudley Philbrick contain the material, which, in the hands of a master, would enrich a romance. But with plain speech, and within a brief space, only the simplest and chiefest facts can be recited.

He was born on the twenty-seventh day of May, in the year eighteen hundred and eighteen. He always marked his birthday by the time of the apple-tree blossoms, which his father had told him were, in this day and year, at their fulness. He was the youngest in a family of three children, having a sister three years older and a brother a year and a half older than himself.

The Philbricks were of a sturdy race of handworkers, possessed of that strength and resolution which come from battling with obstacles. Starting out as pioneers in subduing a new country, all their powers were taxed in winning a subsistence from the soil, and laying by a modest competency for their families. Primarily farmers, the necessities of living in a new country made them

(3)

at the same time carpenters, blacksmiths, and workers in all needed handicraft. They were independent and self-respecting men, but not otherwise distinguished.

Peter Philbrick, the father of John Dudley, was of the third generation which had occupied the homestead farm in Deerfield, N. H., his grandfather, James, having gone there and taken up and cleared the wild land, in the first settlement of the town. Peter was a man of individual character, possessing strong moral qualities and an active intellect, with a decided religious tendency in his nature, and a touch of humor and poetry withal. From his spirituality and power of natural eloquence, he became a leader and exhorting Elder in his church, the Free Will Baptist. In his homestead he possessed a fair country inheritance, but it was burdened with a debt, through some sharpness and dishonesty that had been practiced upon his predecessor. He was an industrious, energetic, and hard-working farmer, but not a thrifty manager, and his devotion to preaching sometimes diverted him from the closest attention to his farm.

With the hope of bettering his situation, he made several removes, locating one year at Epping, another at Stratham, and another at Amesbury, Mass., — when John was from ten to thirteen years of age, — with hardly any other result than enlarging the family horizon, when they again returned to the homestead.

On the maternal side, through his mother, Elizabeth Dudley, he came of a line of strong and fine intellectual fibre. The Dudleys were prominent in the Eastern Colonies from the first settlement of New England, as gov-

ernors, judges, ministers, and lawyers. Mr. Philbrick
was the seventh generation in direct descent, from Gov.
Thomas Dudley of Massachusetts. His great-grand-
father, Judge John Dudley of New Hampshire, for whom
he was named, famous in that State during the period
of the Revolution, was one of the most pronounced char-
acters of his time, — of unswervable integrity, of determined will, of clear foresight, of broad views and sound
judgment. He was not a learned man, nor much read
in books, but Governor Plummer of New Hampshire said
of him that he would sooner trust Judge Dudley's native
faculties to decide a legal point right, than all the lawyers' learning of the other judges put together.

His grandfather, Moses Dudley, was a remarkable type
of the New England country 'Squire of seventy-five years
ago, — wise after the manner of Ben Franklin, — who
gave the last forty years of his life entirely to the study
and reading of books. It was estimated that he had read
the equal of 6,000 octavo volumes of 400 pages each;
and his daily conversation showed the fruits of this great
enrichment.

His mother was a woman of strong mind, well informed, with a determined will, with definite opinions
and the power of expressing them, touched also with an
honest pride of family and with an ambition for position.

Such was the descent and parentage of John Dudley
Philbrick, and he inherited the best and strongest qualities of both lines of his ancestors. In his character, there
was never a better illustration of the logic of heredity.

Deerfield, N. H., lies thirty miles from the coast and

well within the belt of hill country. This whole region is more attractive and picturesque than it is fertile, or productive under cultivation. Nevertheless it is a pleasant country to live in ; but to live, one must work, and the bounds of social and intellectual life, as in all rural towns, are rather narrow. The religious and political newspaper, a few common books, neighborhood visits and gatherings, occasional visits to the market-towns, the town meeting, the schools and church meetings, represent about all.

In this town, in the midst of one of its loveliest valleys, amid surrounding trees, and facing the south, stands the Philbrick homestead, a large main house, made still more ample by the additions of different generations. My personal recollections of it, from the merest boy up to this hour, clothe it with one supreme virtue, — the warm and generous hospitality which it always extended to all comers.

These were the surroundings and this the home of this boy of fifty and sixty years ago.

But here, at this time, the life of a farmer's boy, possessed of imagination and spirit, doubtless, did not seem to the boy to be an ideal one. Yet if somewhat narrow, and unquestionably hard, it held some compensation. It was an open, free, country life, everywhere adapting itself to direct the forces of nature to the uses and comforts of living. On the side of work and on the side of play, it was full of education ; it made ingenious hands, strong arms, swift feet, muscular and well-developed bodies. There was no question here of introducing the new educational factor, industrial training ; the thing *itself* was present in never-ending forms, — the spring's work, the summer's work, the fall and winter's work. When the spring sun began to run high and the fields of snow to melt, the maples were to be tapped and the season's sugar made ; then miles of fence were to be repaired, and the rocks to be picked and hauled from the cultivated fields ; then the dressing was to be hauled and spread upon the land, to be followed by the busy plowing, sowing, and planting. The sheep were to be washed and sheared, providing the wool for home-spinning and weaving, — for the women made all the woolen cloth for clothes, and a surplus to carry and sell in distant markets. The cattle, the horses, the swine, the chickens and turkeys were a constant care. Then commenced the hand to hand contest to keep back the weeds with the hoe, until early July left the crops with a little start in their favor, if rain and sun should be kind.

Then came the midsummer harvest of haying, with no machines to lighten the labor, — mowing, spreading, raking, pitching, hauling, and stowing away, — every stroke one of main strength ; work-days that began before sunrise, and ended with the late dusk of midsummer, — all this for five or six weeks, interrupted only by lowering or rainy weather. Then came cutting the stalks from the corn, reaping the grain with the sickle, gathering and husking the corn, digging and housing the potatoes, gathering the apples, and making the cider ; and the autumn ended with making all the buildings tight and snug for the winter.

In the winter, the season's wood was to be cut and hauled home, and occasionally, logs to be hauled to the saw-mill for boards and lumber, for home use or for the market, — all these things, with the endless daily chores of a farm.

It is at once seen, that being in the midst of a life like this, *early* makes a man out of a boy.

But there were recreations also : a day off fishing or gunning, a trip to the country store, a journey to the market town, a visit to relations or friends, and long winter evenings for reading and talk.

There was also a quiet factor at work, the most important of all, and that was the district school ; this kept three months in the summer and three months in the winter. The boy attended both until he was so large he could no longer be spared from the summer's work, and then went only in winter. But, in the country phrase, "he was a good scholar and loved his books."

And with this education, at sixteen years of age, he was a man.

ACADEMIC LIFE.

But what is there for him beyond this narrow bound of his home ? Where is the opening through which the light can shine ?

To quote his own words : —

" This privilege of going away to school at an academy seemed to be something too high for me ever to dream of enjoying. But in the spring of 1834 some one suggested that I should go to Pembroke Academy, and thus the question was proposed, — Shall I stop with my common school education, or try to get a higher education ? I saw the great difficulty of leaving home, for now I was as good as a man on the farm ; besides, where was the money to come from to pay the expenses ? I did not then imagine it to be possible for me ever to reach the college. But the idea of acquiring an education above that of a common school, found lodgment in my mind, and the idea must become a reality. A young uncle, though six or seven years older than myself, was going to Pembroke to complete his fitting for college. He was to board himself, and kindly offered to take me into the partnership. This fortunate circumstance turned the scale in my favor. My father, who had hesitated to give his consent, not that he did not value education but that he valued my assistance on the farm also, seeing that the opportunity was too good to be lost, yielded, though reluctantly and sadly. I remember the day well. My father, leaving the team standing in the furrow, came into the house to hold a family conference. It must be settled then, for the tailoress was there, and if it was decided in the affirmative, she must be retained to make up the needed garments. My mother said yes, though with some apparent misgivings."

Thus, at sixteen years of age, he went to Pembroke, N. H., for his first term at the Academy. In the four following years he managed to get five or six terms, or parts of terms, of twelve to fourteen weeks, at this school, and one term at Strafford Academy. Between whiles, he returned to the help of his father on the farm, rendered now all the more necessary from the untimely loss of his elder brother, Peter, who died in 1835. This bereavement left a deep and sorrowful mark on his early life.

The brothers were very near of an age, and constant playmates and workmates. This brother was uncommonly bright and of a lovely character. Through life Mr. Philbrick never ceased to mourn this loss, and its anniversary was always a sad day to him. By this blow he became now his father's only dependence, and the difficulty of his absence was accordingly increased, but he still persevered in his course.

His name appears in the Pembroke catalogues of 1834 and 1835, in that of Strafford in 1836, nowhere in 1837, but again in the Pembroke catalogue of 1838. But he was present at these schools only at odd terms.

Pembroke Academy, at this time, was a flourishing and excellent higher seminary, and, with the exception of Phillips Academy at Exeter, one of the best schools in New Hampshire. Its catalogue of 1834, a little pamphlet of eight pages, as big over as your hand, contains 176 names, divided, to use its own words, into " 108 Males and 68 Females." It contains no regular course of study, but names the books, in their order to be studied in preparation for college. It divides the year into three terms, two of fourteen weeks each and one of sixteen weeks. The fee for a certificate of admission is 25 cents. The tuition for the two shorter terms is $4.25, and for the longer term $4.87, with an additional dollar each term to each scholar who studies the French language. The price of board is $1.25 or $1.50 per week, but by walking a moderate distance from the Academy students can be boarded for a less sum.

The catalogues for 1835 and 1836 are substantially the

same. During these three years Joseph Dow was principal. The catalogues of 1837 and 1838, when Isaac Kinsman became principal, show a marked educational advance; three-year courses of study are laid out, term
by term, both for the Male and Female Departments.
Some very pertinent observations are made under the
head of studies and courses. It is interesting to quote a
bit of its plain English : —

"The examination of compositions and the rehearsals
of declamations will each constitute a daily recitation.
The whole school will not attend these recitations together as a class, but in succession, four or five individuals at a time. Each composition will be read by the
teacher, with the writer by his side. It will be scrutinized word by word and sentence by sentence. All its
superfluities and misconceptions, and, so far as possible,
its deficiencies will be pointed out. In oratory, the
scholar will be *drilled.* Tone, inflection, emphasis,
position, motion, if faulty, will be criticised *on the spot.*"

Mr. Kinsman was a thorough and an inspiring teacher,
and as such exerted at this time and afterwards no little
influence over the young student, Philbrick. But the
main motive which led him to persevere at the academy,
and to go on to college, was the same which first started
him in this direction,— the sympathy and encouragement
of the maternal uncle, whom he mentions. This uncle,
in writing to his sister, Mr. Philbrick's mother, in 1838,
says : —

"I am extremely glad that John has manifested so
much determination and decision in pursuing his education ; you can do nothing for him, in my opinion, which

will be of so much real and substantial benefit to him in
after life, and for which he will ever hold you in so grateful remembrance, as to assist and encourage him in this
course.   He must enter college this fall without fail ; if
he goes in debt a few hundred dollars, don't be scared ;
he will be able if he has his health, in one or two years at
most, to clear himself."

The debt of gratitude to this uncle, Elbridge G. Dudley,
afterward a lawyer in this city, was never forgotten.

Writing to his father from Pembroke, May 2, 1835, he
says he appreciates the valuable privileges there enjoyed
of intellectual and moral education, but is aware that they
will not always last, and that, as his father is doubtless
impatiently awaiting his return, he is using every ex-
ertion to accomplish what he can in the little time he
has to stay.   Writing later, he says he regrets that time
should fly so swiftly, and that he has so short a time to
remain.   It appears that this term of his school was to
close, July 30, and his father had expected him to return
home by the Fourth of July, to assist with the haying.
In a letter he pleads to be allowed to remain, if not the
whole term, at least until the 11th, and says he has good
reason to hope that this request will not be denied him.

Such was the continual struggle which covered these
four years.   An odd term or a part of a term at the academy was had, when he could be released from helping at
home, and when a little ready money for expenses could
be gathered together.   To provide a part of this money, he
at this time spent his winters in teaching in the district
schools of his own neighborhood.   In teaching one of

these schools he boarded round. One winter he taught in his home district, where he had lately been a pupil. These schools were attended by the large boys and girls, as well as by the smaller of all ages, and he had pupils as old as or older than himself. I have heard those who were pupils at this school, old men now of seventy, within the past year, tell what a good school he kept and how much he was liked as a master. One told me how he would go out and take part with the boys in the sports, at noon or recess, and how on one occasion he accidentally got a hard hit over the eye with a snowball, so that the eye had to be bandaged for the afternoon. " But," said the old man, " he made nothing of it; I tell you, we liked him."

In 1837 he does not appear to have gone away to school at all; but he taught in the winter of 1836–1837, in the adjoining town of Nottingham. An old pupil from this place, whom he scarcely remembered, writes to him fourteen years after : " Your memory is still dear to the citizens of this district; the school has not flourished since as it did while you were here. Often do I hear your evening school and exhibition spoken of ; they left a deep and abiding impression on the hearts of all who attended them."

In June of this year, 1837, he wrote his uncle saying he had not attended school a single day, not having found any opportunity to leave home ; that it was a source of great anxiety to him that he had been able to make so little progress in literary pursuits, because, he added, " I fear I shall not be able to keep the promise I made you.

I feel unwilling to lose so good an opportunity to go to college. For that reason I have been trying to do all I could at home, but I have labored with only a faint hope of success. I am determined, however, to persevere in the study of the languages till I see you, when I hope the affair will be settled. Cicero and Sallust, I think with a little study I can handle, but Virgil and the Greek Reader will go rather hard."

LIFE AT COLLEGE.

And he did "persevere," and his "faint hope of success" became a hope realized. At twenty years of age, in August, 1838, he successfully presented himself for admission to Dartmouth College. This was a proud day for the struggling student. He says in a letter written at the time: "I went to the president and applied for admission. I was immediately admitted to examination on presenting my recommendation, and was directed to two professors, to have the business "done up." Latin went easy, as well as Algebra, but Greek did not go quite so smooth, though my examination was on the whole by no means a severe one. I, of course, had to promise to make up that part of the Greek Reader I had not read, and also the four Gospels. The others from Pembroke had to do the same."

He at once set about to procure lodgings, and writes that he and his roommate have two very delightful rooms, one of which they used for a sleeping-room, clothes-press, and woodhouse, and the other for a study-room. For their furniture they paid twelve dollars, having determined to get that which was decent and durable. The price of board is \$1.58 per week, or, without tea and coffee, \$1.42. He states that he is highly pleased with his situation, and that his most sanguine expectations are fully realized, and even far excelled. He describes his routine of study, and says a college is the place to learn. Here there are no impediments and every necessary facility ; if the same prosperity which has now dawned, continues, his college course will be a happy one, and if he is permitted to go through, it will be the May-day of his life.

He entered a freshman class of 101, the largest the college had, up to that time, seen. The class contained many bright young men, most of whom had been much more thoroughly prepared than himself. Here he remained throughout the course, availing himself, however, of the permission to be absent winters for the purpose of teaching. These absences were, however, sometimes prolonged in his case, by cutting off from the end of the fall term or the beginning of the spring term. By the money earned in this teaching and by small loans he procured from time to time, he paid his own way throughout the course. The college expenses at that time were not heavy. I observe that those which were classed as necessary, not including contingent, are fixed in the catalogue of 1838, at \$106.24. But there were many contingent expenses, amounting to more, perhaps, than the amount named. In these he practiced the strictest economy. He traveled back and forth from home sometimes by stage, sometimes by private conveyance, and often walked long distances to make these connections. His clothes were made at home, usually out of store cloth, which had been procured by his mother's exchanging homespun of her own make, by carrying it for this purpose thirty miles to a market town.

At this time Dr. Nathan Lord was president of Dartmouth College, a man known for his strong character and wide scholarship; and there was an uncommonly able corps of professors, many of them excellent teachers; Charles B. Hadduck, Alpheus Crosby, Ira Young, Edwin D. Sanborn, O. P. Hubbard, Stephen Chase, and Samuel Gilman Brown.

He had entered college with the highest appreciation of its advantages; the struggle to reach its doors had been long, difficult, and uncertain. He knew what it had cost to get there, he knew how much it would cost to remain, and therefore he valued it. He was determined to make the best use of its every opportunity. He brought with him health, energy, industry, perseverance, courage, and ambition; and as a solid basis for these, integrity and every strong moral quality. What followed was a matter of course; he was a thorough and faithful student, always acquitting himself well in the recitation room, and present at every required exercise.

He also availed himself of every privilege outside of the mere routine. He was active in the literary societies, frequently writing and speaking, and especially ambitious to excel in these respects. In the time left over, he pursued a thorough course of reading, embracing chiefly history, romance, and poetry. This reading he followed up with continuous assiduity in his lengthened absences from the college.

He was by no means indifferent to such recreations and athletic sports as then prevailed among the students. His favorite recreation was walking, for which the country surrounding the college is so inviting ; and he made many excursions among its hills and valleys. In the warm season, swimming in the adjacent Connecticut River was one of the college pastimes, and he became an adept in this art. It is noted by one of his classmates that in swimming a mile stretch, though taken with the cramp, he refused to be taken into the accompanying boat, but " kicked it out." He took pleasure in the military company organized among the students, and from his love of obedience and discipline and his inclination to command, always had a fondness for this service. He was interested also in politics, and near the end of his course was elected president of the college democratic club.

He was an actor in a dramatic incident, which occurred near the close of his junior fall, in the presidential election of 1840. He was now 22 years of age, an ardent democrat, but had never voted. He determined at this time to cast his first ballot. To do this he returned from Hanover to Deerfield, a distance of seventy-five miles by stage, leaving on the last day of October and arriving at Concord, on his way, at half-past one o'clock the same night. He at once set out alone on foot for Deerfield, still twenty miles distant, meeting, as he says, the rising sun on the summit of Prescott's Hill, four miles away, and arriving at home just in season for breakfast. The election was next day, and he was on hand. Party spirit ran high, and the voting list was closely scrutinized by both sides. There was at that time living with his father, as a cheap hired hand, an ignorant but fairly intelligent fellow, named Francis York. He had been brought up in the poorhouse of an adjoining town, but for the past eight years had been self-supporting. The Whig magnate of Deerfield, a lawyer of distinguished family and influence, overawed the selectmen, and induced them to strike York's name from the voting list, on the ground that he was a town pauper. Upon this, young Philbrick stepped up and protested against the act. Amid the great crowd of assembled voters he spoke for eight or ten minutes, with an earnestness that filled them with astonishment. York's name was quickly restored to the list. John went back home, brought York to the town meeting, and saw that he deposited his vote.

"To-day," said he, "has been the most glorious day of my life. I have emancipated a man and defended his rights."

On the whole he stood high at college as a man and scholar, — among the first, — but was not distinguished otherwise than for his sterling qualities. One of his classmates writes that he was not so conspicuous in any respect, compared with the average of his class, as to lead to expectations of his career of distinction. He was unassuming, prompt in his exercises, doing justice to the subject and credit to himself, writes another classmate. Another says he was a resolute, plucky fellow, and upon an attempt made to haze his roommate by some of the sophomores, when he was a freshman, his assailants went down stairs very much in a hurry, followed by sundry billets of wood, and very much worsted. I may add that when this incursion of four masked and cloaked sophomores was made into his room, he was engaged in writing a letter home, which letter I have seen. With the few minutes' interruption necessary to put out the intruders and throw them down stairs, he calmly resumed his writing, with as firm a hand as ever, only incidentally mentioning this little disturbance, and saying that he "pounced upon these fellows like an eagle upon his prey."

Another classmate writes: "The most marked characteristics of all which I remember were his ambition and energy; the former trait led me once to say to him that I thought nothing but the presidency of the United States would satisfy him. There was the same enthusiasm in everything that he undertook at that time that he showed in all his after life. Firm in his opinions and tenacious of his rights, he had also exceeding good-nature and kindness of heart."

His classmate, the Hon. George Walker, now and for a long time, United States Consul General at Paris, in an interesting letter, states: "I remember him particularly well as a steady, studious man of high character and dignified manners. I have the impression that he was a good scholar. I should say that he was a man who was always growing, never rapidly, but assimilating what he learned, and becoming every year that I knew him stronger and more capable of useful work."

Another classmate, Dr. J. Baxter Upham, writes: "Everything he did, was well and thoroughly done. He was a ready speaker and an excellent writer, a good scholar, one of the best in the division in which we were together. He was also noted for his honor, integrity, and straightforwardness. He would not stoop to do a low or mean thing. He also had pluck, boldness, and courage, though he was as gentle and kind as he was brave."

His senior year in college was very much shortened by his prolonged absences for teaching. He left Dartmouth, as he records, early in November of his senior year, without leave or license, and did not return until the last day of the following May. On presenting his excuse to the president for this extended absence, he states that it was immediately accepted and no questions asked. What that excuse was we can readily infer: it was the necessity of earning his own way. Still under this pressure for funds, even now immediately upon his return to college, he was casting about for a location to teach after he should graduate.

It should be said here in explanation of the extreme pressure he felt for earning money, that he not only supported himself at school and college, but helped his sister to obtain a liberal education, and was so keenly sensitive to his filial obligations, that from time to time he provided his father with help upon the farm to compensate for his own necessary absence. Indeed, it was "the custom of the country" for boys to help, and not *be* helped; and money was much more scarce, valuable, and hard to get than it is now.

His mind at this time, as the end of his college course was approaching, was filled with thoughts and plans for the future. His determination and confident expectation from the time he first went away to school up to the close of his senior year in college, had been to study and pursue the profession of the law ; indeed, at this time he had already begun its earnest reading. Returning home from his senior fall, he makes this note on the eleventh of November, 1841 : —

" This evening I kindled a fire in the west room, filled my lamp, seated myself in grandfather's old arm-chair, and commenced in earnest the study of my profession, by reading the forty-fourth chapter of Gibbon's Rome, which treats of Roman jurisprudence."

This study of the law he continued in the leisure hours from his teaching for several years after quitting college, reading all of the elementary and many of the advanced treatises on this science. But though better qualified than most applicants, he never sought admission to the Bar. He did not, however, give up the idea of following this profession, for which he had a strong inclination and many marked qualifications, but fully intended to pursue it, until he became master of the Quincy School, in 1847.

But to return to his outlook from college at the close of his course. His mind was full of projects ; he had a strong inclination to go to Virginia, or some part of the South. He was offered the Yarmouth Academy on Cape Cod ; he was invited to share the management of the Gymnasium, at Pembroke, by Mr. Kinsman. He considered the plan of starting a high school in his native

town. The thing that he most wanted to do was to continue his study of the law, and his plan for this was to
enter the office of Franklin Pierce, at Concord, N. H.

Everything had to give way, however, to the pressing
and immediate need for funds, and he chose the most
promising opening in this respect. Through the friends
he had made at Danvers, Mass., he was now offered a
position as assistant in a private institution, the Roxbury,
Mass., Latin School, which he at once accepted. It is
curious to note that his ancestor, Governor Thomas
Dudley, was one of the chief founders of this school in
1645. Following the matter up immediately, that the
place might be secured beyond contingency, he left
Dartmouth on the last day of June, having remained
there in his senior summer just one month. His last
year in college, therefore, consisted of an attendance
there of about three months only. Under the rules,
owing to these absences, he could not graduate with his
class, but by making up the deficient studies, he was
accorded an examination at the next Commencement,
and given a diploma of the date of his class.

MR. PHILBRICK'S EARLY EXPERIENCE IN TEACHING.

On the principle that one learns by doing, a very important part of Mr. Philbrick's education came from the
relation where he was teacher instead of pupil. As we
have seen, during the course of his preparation for college, and while there, he taught seven winter district
schools and one term at an academy. The primary object had in view was to get funds to pay for his own

schooling, but the secondary object attained was even more important. He was educating himself as well as instructing others, and unconsciously bending his mind in a direction which led to the final choice of his life pursuit.

He taught first in the intervals of his fragmentary attendance at the Academy for two or three successive winters, in the district schools of the vicinity of his home. In his residence at Pembroke Academy, he had become acquainted with several members of the family of Putnam, who came from Danvers, Mass. Led by this acquaintance, and hope of help from it in securing a position, he started out at the end of his freshman fall to look for a school in this town or its vicinity. He had no difficulty in obtaining one through these friends, and was engaged to teach in their own district. This same school he taught for three successive winters. While here, he became acquainted with his fellow-teachers in Danvers and in the near vicinity, especially at Salem. He visited their schools and met them in social meetings, finding among them several superior men. In this old county in Massachusetts, he found a set of schools of much greater excellence than the country schools he had been accustomed to in New Hampshire. He was always very enthusiastic and devoted to whatever he was engaged in, and ambitious, as well, to excel in his work. His uniform and continuous success in managing and instructing inspired him with confidence in his ability, and these surroundings afforded every incitement for him to do his best. He observed and studied the methods in the best schools which he visited, and by himself striving to excel them, became much interested in the subject of education itself. Desiring to improve the schools of his native town, on his return to it, from these winter expeditions, he held meetings in the school-houses of the different districts, and lectured to the people on the subject of common school education, and the last winter of his college course, returned to Deerfield to take charge of the school in one of the largest districts, that he might exemplify the improvements in teaching, which he had learned in Massachusetts. At the close of his school there in February, 1842, he was invited by Mr. Kinsman, his old principal at Pembroke, to take the place of assistant in the new Gymnasium there, which Mr. Kinsman had started as a secession from the old academy. He accepted this position, remaining at Pembroke until the last of May, before returning again to college. He made so marked a success in this place, that two or three years later, upon the place of principal becoming vacant, he was invited by the trustees to occupy it, which offer, however, he was not able to accept.

This comprised the whole course of his teaching, while he was engaged in his own school and college studies. It had aroused his mind to the importance of this pursuit, and in becoming a teacher, he had learned the great lesson of how to become a student ; and in his associations in Essex County, he found himself a part of a teaching fraternity, and of a social society, which in intelligence and cultivation, exceeded everything in his previous experience, and these influences left a deep impression upon him.

It was here too, and in the old and honored family of Putnams, that he formed an attachment which had great influence for good on his future; and on the 24th of August, 1843, while teaching in Roxbury, he married Miss Julia A. Putnam of Danvers. The union proved a most happy one, and thus for forty-three years he had the cherishing support of a true *helpmeet,* and the comfort and joy of an ideal home.

TEACHING IN ROXBURY AND BOSTON.

In any complete account of Mr. Philbrick's education and growth, there must be mentioned his first five years of teaching in Roxbury and Boston. Beginning as an assistant in a private school in Roxbury, upon leaving college in 1842, he successively filled various positions, always exchanging a good place for a better one, until, in 1847, he reached the Mastership of the Quincy School, that first united and complete grammar school, which marked so important an era in the school system of Boston.

It was not until this time, I think, that he had discovered his full abilities in the line of education, or had appreciated the importance and vastness of this subject, and its moral incentives for a high career.

His intellectual, moral, and social growth during his college course had been very great, but during this five-year period it was hardly less than marvelous. Coming as a young man from the country into the quick intellectual life of a cultivated city, and by his surroundings thrown into congenial and intelligent society, through his keenness and aptness he assimilated all that was best. Here he found a new education; the college had enlarged itself into a city, and the city again into a world. In his apprenticeship in teaching he owed much to Thomas Sherwin, Master of the English High School in Boston, where he was for two years as assistant.

But the one man to whom he owed more than to all others, in this time, was Dr. George Putnam, then minister of the Unitarian Church in Roxbury. The preaching and teachings of this great man, whose friendship and confidence had been secured by the solid and attractive qualities of this young man, and his influence in close personal intercourse, left a deep and lasting impression upon Mr. Philbrick's character. The determined ambition with which he had started out to pursue and obtain the most obvious prizes of life was transformed into a lofty ambition to attempt only the most worthy objects, and to pursue a course which, first of all, should be of benefit to mankind.

CONCLUSION.

Thus his love of teaching, his eminent success in it, the gradual opening out of its great possibilities, lighted up by this new ambition, led him to adopt the profession of Education as a life career.

With his schooling in the little country district, with his severe training upon the farm, continuing at intervals up to the age of twenty-four; with his academic life, struggled and fought for and obtained in fragments; with his college course, full of patient, industrious, and successful study ; with his eight terms of teaching, stretching through nearly as many years ; with his first five years of teaching in Roxbury and this city, so full of opportunity and culture, — we find him at length standing, a young man of twenty-nine, equipped for his life work, at the head of the first united grammar school in the city of Boston.

In the ripeness of his manhood he looked back upon this formative period of his youth through the fine, ideal glow of distance, — its adversities, its struggles, its triumphs, — as a thing wholly apart from himself ; but every aspiring youth, — nay, the whole human family of children, — was to him the type of this striving boy, reaching out for instruction and knowledge, while his was the duty to answer this call, by upbuilding and establishing the wisest methods of a broad education.

Life and Character

of

JOHN DUDLEY PHILBRICK.

———•———

By Larkin Dunton, LL. D. .

LIFE AND CHARACTER

OF

JOHN D. PHILBRICK.

———•—•———

John Dudley Philbrick was born in Deerfield, New Hampshire, May 27, 1818. He was the son of Elder Peter Philbrick, a clergyman of the Freewill Baptist denomination, and Betsey Dudley.

He fitted for college at Pembroke Academy, in Pembroke, New Hampshire, with the exception of two terms spent in study at Strafford, New Hampshire. He was graduated from Dartmouth College in 1842.

He was a teacher in the Roxbury Latin School, at Roxbury, now a part of Boston, in 1842 and 1843. He was made a teacher in the English High School in Boston in 1844, and the next year was chosen principal of the Mayhew School in Boston, which position he occupied till elected master of the then new grammar school in Boston, called the Quincy School, in 1847. He served as master there from 1847 to 1852.

During the early years of his teaching in Boston, he studied law to some extent, and, contrary to the com. monly expressed opinion, it was not till 1847, the year that he took charge of the Quincy school, that he decided to adopt education as a profession.

He was called from Boston to the State Normal School at New Britain, Connecticut, and served there as principal in 1853 and 1854. He was superintendent of the public schools of the State of Connecticut in 1855 and 1856.

He was superintendent of the public schools of Boston, from December 22, 1856, to September 1, 1874, and from March 1, 1875, to March 1, 1878.

He was agent of the Massachusetts State Board of Education during a part of 1875–1876, in charge of the preparation of the Exhibition of the Education and Science of the State at the Centennial Exposition at Philadelphia ; Massachusetts Special Commissioner of Education, and United States Honorary Commissioner, and Member of the International Jury, at the Vienna Exposition in 1873 ; and Director of the United States Exhibition and Member of the International Jury, at the Paris Exposition, in 1878.

He was at different times one of the editors of the *Massachusetts Teacher.* He was also editor of the *Connecticut Common School Journal* for two or three years, when employed in that State.

The following are among his published works : — Annual Reports of the Public Schools of the State of Connecticut for 1855 and 1856; twelve quarterly and thirty-three semi-annual Reports of the Public Schools of Boston, and several special reports relating to these schools, printed in the annual volumes of the Reports of the School Committee of Boston from 1857 to 1878

inclusive ; the Reports of the Massachusetts State Board
of Education to the Legislature for the years 1865 and
1872; Report as Director of the United States Exhibition at the Paris Exposition of 1878, printed with Reports of the Commissioner in Chief; article *Etats Unis,*
Dictionaire de Pedagogie Paris ; several lectures and
papers printed in the volumes of the American Institute
of Instruction, of the National Educational Association,
and circulars of the National Bureau of Education ;
articles for the *Atlantic Monthly* and *North American*
Review, 1881 ; Catalogue of the United States Exhibition
at Paris, 1878 (pp. 124), London : printed at the Ches-
wich Press; American Union Speaker (pp. 588), Boston,
1865, and second edition (pp. 536), Boston, 1876; the
Primary Union Speaker (pp. 110), Boston ; City School
Systems in the United States, published by the Bureau
of Education, 1885 ; and School Reports printed in the
Proceedings of the Council, 1885.

I am not certain that the list is complete ; but it does
not include a considerable number of unpublished lectures and addresses.

Dr. Philbrick was president of the Connecticut State
Teachers' Association, the Massachusetts State Teachers' Association, the American Institute of Instruction,
and the National Educational Association. He was a
member of the National Council of Education, member
of the Massachusetts Board of Education for ten years,
member of the government of the Institute of Technology from its establishment in 1861 to the time of his
death, and a trustee of Bates College for ten years.

He received the degree of LL.D. from Bates College in 1872, and from St. Andrew's University, Scotland, in 1879; was made Chevalier of the Legion of Honor, France, 1878, and also received the Gold Palm of the University of France, with the title *Officier d' Instruction Publique.*

Probably none of these titles and their accompanying diplomas afforded him so much pleasure as a " Reward of Merit," received from his first teacher, who occupied the "little red schoolhouse on the hill," in School District No. 1, in his native town. Dr. Philbrick remembered this school district in his will. A quarter part of the income from the money which he has left to the town of Deerfield is to be given annually to this district, "in addition to its legal share of school money." The reward of merit read as follows :—

This may certify that John Philbrick is at the head of class No. 2, and for his good behavior and laudable improvement the week past has the approbation of his teacher,
                                        RUTH BAILEY.
Deerfield, July 2, 1824.

His foreign travels in 1873 included visits to Liverpool, London, Paris, Vienna, Prague, the principal cities of Germany, and Brussels; and in 1878, France, England, and Scotland.

Such are the positions he held, the works he wrote, and the marks of honor he received. Let us now examine with more care some of the results of his labors.

Like many of the older teachers of New England, he laid the foundation for his future success in the old district school. He taught in such a district in the town of Danvers, Massachusetts, several winters while in college. Here he was noted for his devotion to his school, and for his interest in a small society of teachers of the town, mostly college students like himself, who used to meet in various parts of the town for mutual help in regard to their professional work. The lessons of professional help from association and conference that he here learned from experience, he never forgot. Perhaps there is not a man in this country who has contributed so largely of time, travel, and talent to the various associations of teachers in the country as our lamented friend. With what patience, and interest, too, he listened to the essays and discussions of others. For he welcomed free interchange of views as the best means of clarifying one's own mind. He was the most sincere lover of criticism, even adverse criticism, that I have ever known. How often I have heard him say, " We should be thankful for the criticisms of our enemies; for our enemies will tell us our faults, a thing which our friends are reluctant to do."

Then what deference he always paid to the opinions of those whose wisdom and experience entitled them to consideration. He had no patience with educational charlatanism; but for a sincere student, for honest experience, his respect was genuine. How many of us have been encouraged to excel ourselves by his appreciative consideration of our opinions based on careful observation. This spirit made him both a teacher and a learner at our conventions.

Of Dr. Philbrick's work in Connecticut I will let Charles Northend speak : —

"He came here [New Britain] in 1852, at the request of Dr. Barnard, to take charge of the State Normal School, a position he filled with rare ability and success. Some two years later, Dr. Barnard resigned the State superintendency of schools, and, on his recommendation, Mr. Philbrick was made State Superintendent of Schools and principal of the Normal School. Of him at this time Dr. Barnard wrote to the president of the State Teachers' Association as follows : 'Mr. Philbrick is a wise, practical teacher, of large personal experience in every department of the educational field, and has shown himself willing to labor 'in season and out of season,' and to 'spend and be spent' in the cause of popular education. He enjoys the highest respect and love of the teachers, and by his ability, common sense, and devotion to his duties will deserve and secure the confidence and co-operation of the people of the State.'

"Mr. Philbrick remained in this State about five years, greatly to the benefit of the Normal School and to the cause of education throughout the State, and when, in 1857, he resigned his position here to accept the superintendency of the schools of Boston, it was greatly to the regret of the friends of progress in school work ; but brief as his stay was here, he was instrumental of great and lasting good.

"I will close this article by naming two or three particulars in which Dr. Philbrick excelled, and to which his great usefulness and eminent success were largely owing :

"1. He was a perfect gentleman, — always courteous, and kind, and winning in his manner, by which he both made and retained friends.

"2. He was a man of great earnestness, sound common

sense, and good judgment ; a man of great firmness and persistent effort in the execution of his views and plans.

" 3. Dr. Philbrick had the rare faculty of gaining the good-will and hearty co-operation of all in any way associated with him. He always most cheerfully accorded to all their full share of merit for what they did, and inspired them with the feeling that he was their true friend."

Dr. Philbrick's first important work in Boston was in making the Quincy school a success. To understand the significance of this work, we must remember that the organization of this school, under Mr. Philbrick, was the beginning of a new departure in school management in the city. Up to that time, 1847, the old "double headed" organization had prevailed. "By this singular arrangement each school had two departments, called the reading and writing departments. Each of these departments was accommodated in a separate apartment ; each had its separate set of studies ; the programme of studies being divided for this purpose, not horizontally by grades, but vertically by subjects ; each had its master and corps of assistants, usually two or three in number ; and the pupils attended each in turn, changing from one to the other at each half-daily session." The pupils all assembled and prepared their lessons in the room with the master. This room usually had a seating capacity of about one hundred and eighty. Originally, all the recitations were conducted in the same room, the master hearing one section of pupils and the assistants hearing the others.

By the arrangement adopted in the Quincy school,

each division was to occupy a separate room ; and when one reflects upon the old state of harshness in discipline, repression, confusion, and corporal punishment, that were necessary, and then upon the quiet, the order, and the kindness of spirit, that would be infused into a school under the new system, he will at once understand why it was so important that the new plan should succeed. Then there were the economic reasons, the reasons that were more potent in the minds of many of the school committee at that time than the pedagogic ones.

Mr. Philbrick proved to be the right man for the new scheme. He made it such a success that, in a few years, the old double-headed system had entirely disappeared ; and no more schoolhouses in Boston have been built on the old plan. Whether the old system would have con- tinued much longer in the event of his failure, it is im- possible to say ; but it is quite evident that the better era was much hastened by his wise and efficient administra- tion. The influence of this change is now felt, perhaps, in every State in the Union ; if not in the structure of schoolhouses, certainly in the mildness of the discipline that has been made possible.

Another great service rendered to the Boston schools, and, indeed, to the schools of the whole country, was the reform in the school programmes. The accomplishing of this required the highest wisdom and the application of the best common sense. Dr. Philbrick had the good judgment, in this as in many other things, to proceed slowly. Even after he knew the right, he took time to do the work necessary for its introduction.

The making of a good programme is undoubtedly the highest kind of pedagogical work. It is easy to tinker a programme, easy to say, "Put this into the schools, and take that out"; but to know the end of human development, its successive stages, its breadth, the relative proportion of each element to be introduced, — to know the means to be used, the matter to be presented, the order of presentation, the proper proportion of time to give to this or that subject; and then to be able to state intelligibly all the processes in proper co-ordination and subordination, — in short, to determine just what shall be done, when and how, by the children of a city, so that all shall be educated in the best way, — this requires pedagogical skill of the highest order. It requires educational wisdom of no mean quality to know enough not to attempt the task.

I doubt whether a greater advance in the constructing of a good programme has been made in this country than was made by Mr. Philbrick in the arranging of the course of study for the primary and grammar schools of Boston. In speaking of the effect of the programme of the primary schools twenty years after it went into operation, he says: "The adoption of this programme was of so much importance as to constitute an era in the history of the primary schools. Its beneficial effects were soon apparent, and they have gone on increasing ever since. It gives definiteness of aim to the teachers which they did not before have, promotes unity and harmony of effort on the part of teachers of different classes, and tends to secure uniformity of progress in corresponding classes in different parts of the city, while it affords at once a standard and guide in making examinations for promotion."

This work of Dr. Philbrick has sometimes been spoken of as though it was, in his mind, an end ; or, at least, that school organization was an end, and not a means. Those who make such criticisms fail to take into account, in the first place, the fact that the making of a good programme implies a profound knowledge of education, both philosophic and practical, and in the second place, the fact that, when his programme was made and well applied in the schools under his control, he began to study the ways and means of raising the teachers under his direction to the rank of educational philosophers with as much zeal as he had ever displayed in the construction or introduction of the programme.

It was just at this point that he was misunderstood by his critics. Because he laid a necessary foundation first, and then sought means for erecting the superstructure, it was assumed that he would never build. Shrewdly has Dr. White remarked, " His apparent conservatism was the poise of deep insight and wide knowledge." While others would fail on account of moving too soon, he could wait till all contingencies were provided for.

Another important service rendered by Dr. Philbrick was the making of the grammar masters principals of districts. The primary schools of Boston remained un-graded down to 1856; but between that date and 1864 they had been graded into six classes, and, when practicable, a single class was assigned to each teacher. This arrangement, of course, required promotions to be made every six months, from one primary teacher to another, unless the teachers were sent from grade to grade with their pupils, a plan which was not generally adopted. " This made it necessary that some one should be charged with the responsibility of supervising the group with reference to the admission of pupils, their proper classification, and their qualifications for promotion, from class to class, and to the grammar schools."

At the same time the number of pupils in each of the grammar schools had become so much larger under the "single-headed" organization that an improvement in the supervision of the lower classes had come to be felt as a necessity. The master was occupied in teaching the first class, and consequently the labors of the subordinate teachers were often undirected, or misdirected, and, consequently, conflicting in their aims. This laid the foundation for " high pressure " in the first class, for the pupils often came up poorly qualified to do the work required. And the more the master tried to remedy the deficiency in his own class, the more he was increasing the evil for the succeeding class by neglecting the classes below. And, beside, the pupils who left school without reaching the first class received little benefit from the superior experience and teaching power of the master.

To remedy all these evils, Dr. Philbrick conceived the plan of relieving the master from the duty of teaching in the first class, and of making him the principal, not only of the grammar school, but of all the primary schools in his district as well. This scheme had the ever potent

merit of cheapness ; and, after a long discussion, and the
support of an able report, it was adopted by the Board.
The conservative members, however, succeeded in adding
a modification to the original plan, to the effect that the
new duty of the master should be performed "under the
direction of the district committee." This qualification
wrought much harm in some districts for a long time, but
in the main the plan soon went into effect.

Nearly ten years later Dr. Philbrick writes : —

" This measure has unified the whole system and
greatly increased its strength and efficiency. Without it
the new programme would have proved little better than
so much waste paper. Each master is now not merely a
teacher of one small class, — *he is the training master and
real director of all the classes in his district.* If he does
his duty he teaches more or less in every class to show
how they should be handled, and so aids and directs the
teachers in carrying out the programmes, that their labor
may, as far as possible, contribute to the accomplishment
of the desired objects."

But I must hasten on, for time would fail me to treat,
with anything like fullness, of all the reforms wrought
in the Boston schools, through the wise foresight and
patient labor of Dr. Philbrick.

He kept the school expenditures from being reduced
to a point that would cripple the efficiency of the schools.
He never boasted of cheap schools. The farthest he
ever went in this direction was to show the people that
school expenses, in the time of high prices, were not increased so rapidly as other city expenses, and that for

the most extravagant use of money for school purposes
the school committee were not responsible; but he never
so far yielded to the popular clamor for retrenchment as
to consent to the reduction of teachers' salaries, or the
cheapening of the necessary supplies for the schools.
He saw clearly that the schools must cost money if they
were to be good, and his motto was, "Schools good
enough for the rich are poor enough for the poor." If
the public schools are patronized by the wealthy they are
economical, even for them, and so Mr. Philbrick sought
to make the public schools better than it is possible to
make private schools.

His wise counsels were felt in the construction of
schoolhouses. Mr. George A. Clough, the able architect
of the Latin and English High School building in Boston, says : —

"The earliest impressions that I received upon school
architecture were from Dr. Philbrick, as far back as 1871,
and now, after fifteen years' experience, I have had an
opportunity to see that his views were far in advance of
all other writers upon the subject in this country. In
reviewing my experience I find myself constantly associated with the early views of Dr. Philbrick."

In the matter of school furniture such a change was
wrought under his administration that the effect has
been felt all over this country, and even in other countries. To his wisdom are we, perhaps, mainly indebted
for the use of a single desk for every scholar, from the
primary school to the high.

He was among the first, — perhaps the very first, — of

the leading educators of the country to perceive the value of art education, and to take steps toward its promotion. Mr. John S. Clark, of the firm of Prang & Co., a man as well qualified to speak upon this point as any man in the United States, says : —

" The movement for the study of drawing in the public schools . . . . had its beginning in Boston. I do not think I do injustice to the many gentlemen who took a deep interest in starting the movement in Massachusetts when I say that the leading spirit in the movement was Dr. Philbrick. In my various consultations with him he surprised me, not only by the thoroughness of his observation of what had been done abroad, but also by his clear comprehension of what was necessary to be done here before any success could be expected. To Dr. Philbrick more than to any other one person are we indebted for our Massachusetts Normal Art School. It was through his instrumentality, mainly, that Mr. Walter Smith was induced to come to Boston in 1872."

And, I may add that the influence of this movement upon the industrial productions and upon the artistic tastes of the people of this country is beyond computation.

In the department of vocal music great progress was made during Dr. Philbrick's administration. When he took charge of the schools, in 1856, singing was indifferently taught in only a portion of the classes of the grammar schools, and in these it was not taught by the regular teachers. In fact, " there was no prescribed programme of instruction, no harmony of methods, no uniformity of textbooks, no classification, — in fact, no system." At the close of his connection with the schools, a thorough, systematic, and progressive course of musical instruction was given to all the pupils, beginning with the youngest on their entrance into school, and ending with the last year of the high school course; and there was, also, a systematic course of instruction given to the pupils of the Boston Normal School to qualify the students to teach music when they should be called to take charge of classes as teachers.

Dr. Philbrick, as long ago as 1860, took strong ground in favor of the introduction of physical training, or gymnastics, into the public schools. After much opposition, the plan that he proposed in 1860 was adopted in 1864, and a special teacher of vocal and physical culture was appointed. Not so much has been accomplished in this department in Boston as is needed, on account of our lack of facilities. The difficulty of improvement in this branch of instruction is a good illustration of the conservative force of an established order of things. To make physical culture really effective, a gymnasium is necessary in connection with each school, and in Boston the schoolhouses are so situated that the acquisition of ground for suitable buildings would be very expensive; and so even those who are wise enough to see the need of such buildings hesitate to move in the matter.

The plan at present in operation in Boston of employing a force of truant officers by the school committee was developed during Dr. Philbrick's administration. At first truant officers were appointed by the mayor and aldermen, and were not responsible to the school com-

mittee for the performance of their duty. They for a
long time met the superintendent once a month as a
matter of courtesy, but not as a duty. At last the authority to appoint these officers and fix their salaries was
conferred upon the school committee by general statute,
and then they met the superintendent once a week for
consultation and direction. After this system had been
developed and perfected by a series of experiments in
Boston, its beneficial effects were so marked that it attracted the attention of other American cities, and finally
produced much effect in England and other foreign countries. The action of the truant force in Boston was so
moulded by the superintendent that the moral influence
of the officers in promoting a better state of feeling
toward the schools, among ignorant parents, and thus
securing greater regularity of attendance, was, perhaps,
quite as great as that of their direct, legally required
work.

Outside the public schools Dr. Philbrick's influence
was constantly felt for good. He was a member of the
association that secured the charter of the Massachusetts
Institute of Technology. From the day of the chartering
of this institution to the day of his own death he was a
member of the corporation and of the committee on instruction. He was a constant attendant of the meetings, both of the corporation and of the committees to
which he belonged, and, by his labors and counsel, did
much to develop this important institution.

He was no inconsiderable factor in the forces that created the Boston Museum of Fine Arts. He was the first

temporary secretary of this association, and did much to secure the necessary funds for its establishment. Many of those who listen to me to-day will remember his personal influence in this direction.

His last work for Boston, as well as for the rest of the country, was his great argument in favor of a permanent tenure of office for teachers. His lecture upon this subject before the American Institute of Instruction, and his masterly treatment of the same in his report to the Commissioner of Education upon city school systems, did much toward securing the passage of the act by the Legislature last winter, which confers upon school committees authority to dispense with the annual re-election of teachers, — a movement which, in the opinion of Dr. Philbrick, is second to no reform in education that has been inaugurated in this country.

But, were I called upon to single out from all the grand achievements of Dr. Philbrick in Boston, the one more potent than all the rest, the one stronger and more far-reaching in its influence than all others, the one that has done most to make the Boston schools known and honored wherever public schools exist in the whole world, the one that is destined, unless destroyed by narrowness and jealousy, to exert the strongest influence in the improvement of our schools in the future, I should name, not schoolhouses, not school furnishings, not programmes, not methods, not special schools, not even the diffusion of a sound philosophical spirit, but rather the creation of a higher ideal of the schoolmaster's office, — an ideal that makes the office respected and honored by the people, and that makes the school itself the master's pride and glory, and the object of his entire consecration and devotion. This was the crowning glory of Dr. Philbrick's work in Boston.

One of the fundamental philosophical principles that was early developed in Dr. Philbrick's mind, and that became a guiding force in many of his reforms, was the truth that specialized functions require specialized agencies. As soon as it became evident to him that there was a special work to be done he at once began to cast about for the proper agency for its accomplishment. Hence we find growing up in Boston, under his wise guidance, and developing under his fostering care, evening elementary schools, evening high schools, evening drawing schools, schools for licensed minors, a deaf-mute school, in addition to the regular primary, grammar, and high schools. The same principle, also, held him as a firm advocate of the establishment of a separate Latin school for girls, instead of having the work of fitting girls for college done in the regular high school for girls where the chief business is giving a general education.

The application of this principle compelled him to take ground in favor of a separate and distinct normal school. He saw, with the insight of a sage, that the work of preparing young women to become teachers in primary and grammar schools was, in its finishing process, entirely distinct from the general work of developing scientific and literary power, and, therefore, as he believed, a special agency should be employed for performing this special work. I remember well a visit to the Boston Normal

School by the superintendent of schools of New York, — Mr. Kiddle, — soon after the separation of the Normal School from the Girls' High. We were then just struggling into existence; but, after witnessing the work of the school for some time, he remarked, " You have the right organization, — a special school for special work."

And yet this is only a single instance of the profoundly philosophic mould of Dr. Philbrick's mind. He told me, within a few years of his death, that he had never written a sentence on education that he would wish to blot. It is remarkable to observe what unity and consistency run through all his writings. The reason of this is obvious to those who know the deep principles that ran through all his educational thinking and unified all his educational work. Dr. Harris well expressed this fact when he said, " His annual reports were luminous with insight into the relations of practical methods to the history of pedagogy. He was a city set upon a hill. He never wrote a paragraph without considering the relation of its doctrine to the theory and practice of the world."

The ability to do this implies what we all concede, that he was profoundly versed in educational history. Some have attempted to separate a knowledge of educational philosophy from that of educational practice, and to attribute to him the latter, but to deny him the former; but those who so estimate the man know him only in part. He was, indeed, deeply read in systems of school organization, but these systems lay in his mind as the development of corresponding philosophies. He was strong as a practical school man, but the secret of his

practical strength lay in his profound knowledge of the
principles that determine right practice.

This made him conservative. While others were ready
to embrace a newly presented theory or method, he felt
compelled to hesitate. He must first consider whether it
had not already been properly tested and rejected, and
whether or not it was in accordance with those principles
that he held as fundamental. Often would he reject a
method of teaching which, for the time being, was popular, well knowing that it was not in accordance with the
views of the wisest educators. If any new, really new,
method was proposed, he always inquired, before he accepted it, whether it was in accordance with the tendency
of the best practice of the world. But few men could
apply this test. He had the necessary knowledge, and it
gave him great strength. He was so well versed in pedagogical history that he knew what the various nations of
the world had formerly done, what they were now doing,
and the changes both in theory and practice through
which they were going. And he judged that, if all the
most enlightened nations of the world were moving in a
given direction, that direction, while not necessarily absolutely right, was more likely to be right than any
course that could be thought out by one single mind.
How many times I have heard him say, " This practice
is wrong because it is contrary to the unanimous opinion
of the wisest educators." This test he often applied
with wonderful skill.

It has been said of him that he was not a great man.
But what is the standard of greatness? This is a relative

term, of course. No one talent of his overshadowed all the rest; but his mind was well rounded and evenly balanced, and one of remarkable force. His power of application was wonderful. His classmate, Rev. Dr. Spalding, says of him, "No man in college was more noted for his indefatigable industry." And the habit thus early formed clung to him till the day of his death. His judgment of men was excellent, and his opinion of the best means to secure a desired end was rarely wrong. His view of a broad truth was clear to a degree attained by but few, and his power to apply general principles to special cases was equal to his power of insight. If greatness be judged by success, we must accord it to him in no small degree. Few men of a generation impress themselves upon the world so strongly or so widely. Probably no school man lives to-day who is so widely and so favorably known as was Dr. Philbrick at the time of his death.

Not only the esteem in which he was held by educators, but the affection they felt for him, was unusual. What is the secret? Is it not to be found partly in the fact that his highest ambition was to be of real service to mankind? In the seclusion and sacredness of his own study, July 9, 1865, he wrote : —

"I often urge as the chief end of man, self-culture, with a view to use talents and acquirements for the benefit of others. I got a glimpse of this great idea while in college, I know not how, and it grew and expanded till it came to be my guiding principle. It was this which at length determined my choice of a profession. I felt that

the educational field was that in which I could best develop my own character and at the same time do the
most good to mankind. I expected labor and trials, but
these are necessary for culture. I have no regret on
account of my choice; I only regret that I have not *done*
more. Not but that I have worked hard enough, but I
have not always worked to the best advantage. To accomplish great things one must have great power of
endurance and also great wisdom to direct his efforts, so
that he may always work to the best advantage."

The desire to do the most good to mankind determined
the choice of his profession! Have we not here the key
to that cheerful and unruffled patience with which he
continually worked, to his catholic charity toward those
who delayed the accomplishment of his cherished plans,
and to that sweet spirit of Christian forgiveness of his
enemies that made him so lovable in the quiet retirement
of his later years? How constantly he was guided by
this principle those know best who knew him most. In
his view education was a high and holy calling, worthy of
the ambition of the noblest minds, and to this he consecrated his life.

His integrity never faltered. Honesty, both intellectual and moral, was a native element of his character.
Selfish aims and ambitions found no lodgment in his
heart. He preferred failure to insincerity.

Then he was generous and sympathetic. No man was
quicker to detect merit in others or more ready to give
credit where it was due. How many have been cheered
by his kind words of sympathy and his wise counsels.
He was a real friend to all who were honestly working
for the good of public schools.

Able and industrious, devoted to his profession, and a student of its history and philosophy, sincere, generous, and sympathetic, patient and forgiving, his life was a grand success. Wherever public schools exist his influ-ence is felt ; wherever popular education is studied he is known. His mind was clear and strong ; his character was round, and full, and sweet ; and his life contributed abundantly to the good of mankind. Long may his memory live in our heart of hearts, and long may his noble example inspire us to emulate his virtues, and to consecrate ourselves, head and heart, soul and body, to the great work to which he devoted his life.

Public Services

of

JOHN DUDLEY PHILBRICK.

By W. T. Harris, LL. D.

PUBLIC SERVICES

OF

JOHN D. PHILBRICK.

We honor and esteem the development of human character above all other products of this world. We do not value possessions so much as being. Character is not the indifferent foundation of the soul which is capable of becoming either good or bad, but it is the positive structure that is erected on that foundation. Hence, we speak of a good man as a man of character, and of a bad man we say that he has no character.

Again, it is evident that character is never the product of external circumstances; it is formed only by the reaction of the human will against these circumstances. It is always the product of the self-activity of the man himself. He reacts upon the world around him, and moulds it by his will. In proportion as he attains power to realize what is rational in this world he attains character. Looking upon each individual as a possibility of this precious outcome, we must value most highly any instrumentalities which tend to favor its growth and development. All doings and havings which do not appertain to the growth of human character fail in an essential particular. They do not have any part or lot in what is eternal. Only the going forth of the soul in the image of its Maker is of prime importance in the affairs of this world, and all deeds and events take rank according to their near or remote relation to this essential purpose.

In view of this principle, we assemble to recount the evidences of character in our great men after they have gone from us. What they have done for us, what they have done for their fellow-men, is the test of this substantial growth in themselves. For, strangely enough in human life, it is true that one finds his deepest self in the recognition that he receives from society. He works for it by working for others. It is the Christian doctrine that he who wishes to save his life in an immediate and selfish manner shall lose it ; and he who loses his life for the sake of others, he alone gains it; he obtains a hold on his true being, — he realizes character.

It is thus with the noble educator whom we celebrate on this occasion. Early in life, as we have heard from those who were most intimate with him, he consecrated himself to the work which promised the most direct field of usefulness to his fellow-men. There opened before him many careers of honor and success, — careers, indeed, that promised honor and wealth at a far less outlay of endeavor. But he perceived that easily won honors are not enduring ones ; he perceived that, in the long run, it is only character that is honored, and character builds itself by heroic self-sacrifice for the good of humanity. The missionary spirit, the zeal of St. Francis of Assisi, the zeal of St. Paul, the apostle to the gentiles, the zeal

of the noble army of Christian missionaries, is the type
of this highest unfolding of the human soul, for it is the
nearest approach to the Divine Model as revealed to us
in Christ.

Looking at human welfare in its broadest sense, we
shall agree, I think, in this: The highest service to men
is that which brings to bear upon them the influence that
will fill them with the spirit of self-sacrifice for the good.
Character is that which develops character in others.
Next after the heroes who preach the gospel of the highest religion to men come the teachers who open the windows of the intellect and let the light of science into
the soul.

In a world full of sin and evil, full of poverty and suffering, full, likewise, of discontent and mutiny against
established order, what is the first and best gift that one
can offer to his day and generation? Certainly, we shall
say, next after the teachers who teach religion come the
secular teachers who teach science and enlighten the intellect, while they train the will into moral habits.

Take the evils of society, poverty, vice, disease, and
crime, and consider their suppression and cure. The administration of justice, the dispensing of charity, do much
to punish or cure, but very little to prevent. It is the
opinion of many wise and thoughtful people that charity
is often so managed that it aggravates evil by increasing
its producing causes. To the social economist, however,
one way is clear, — school education is a powerful preventive. It increases the productive power of the individual by increasing his directive intelligence and by

increasing his power of will, for the school rests on three pillars : First, the cultivation of the habit of industry, the will-power to do its reasonable task whether it is easy, pleasant, and agreeable, or difficult and disagreeable. Second, the training of the intellect into science, the giving it possession of the tools of thought, the mastery of written and printed language in which is revealed human nature ; the mastery of arithmetic and its kindred branches, in which are revealed the laws and conditions of matter ; and such studies as give insight into the structure of reason, like grammar, or into the growth of human institutions, like history, or into our present relations to all mankind, like geography. Thirdly, there is the training into habits of courtesy and morality, the great lesson of civil life, the combination with one's fellow-men in peaceful forms of helpfulness, and the suppression of animal tendencies to strife and contention. The school teaches pupils to meet each other and cooperate to secure a reasonable end by courteous and considerate behavior. In fact, the humblest and most elementary school, as well as the highest and most advanced school, does something to contribute to individual and social welfare. It teaches the individual to help himself and to combine helpfully with his fellow-men. In an age of rapid changes in industry and in social conditions, it is indispensable that the individual shall be educated into the power to adapt himself to his circumstances, the power to readjust himself in case of emergencies. All will acknowledge that industry, the mastery of knowledge, and the tools of thought and courteous behavior are the most essential requisites for this age of change and transition.

While, therefore, we gladly recognize the nobility of a life devoted to commerce and trade, to manufactures, to agricultural production, or to the professions of law and medicine, yet we must feel the weight of the motives which moved Mr. Philbrick, when a serious-minded and ambitious young man, to select the vocation of teacher. Such motives the half-conscious, half-unconscious stuff of feelings and aspirations moved his great contemporaries, Horace Mann, Henry Barnard, Thomas Arnold, George Peabody, Johns Hopkins, to devote life, or fortune, or both, to the cause of education. Here is the field where charity will make no mistakes ; here is the field where justice will prevent, as well as suppress and cure crime and vice and pauperism. The productive power of an educated community surpasses that of an uneducated community, not threefold merely, but three hundred fold. The trained intellect can invent and bring to its aid the forces of nature. The pupil trained to perform his task without a murmur, when the subject is difficult and dis- tasteful, — being far remote from his daily interests and objects of life, — has conquered his selfish appetites and has learned self-government, and thereby become fit to govern others.

We have already listened to the reminiscences of Mr. Philbrick's youth, and learned the story of his aspirations and his struggles. We have heard, too, of his special work here in Boston, first as assistant teacher, and next as principal teacher or head master ; then, finally, as

general superintendent of the entire school system of
Boston. It remains now for me to attempt a brief
summary of his significance to the cause of education in
general. I have, therefore, begun what I had to say by
calling your attention to the position which the cause of
popular education holds in human life as a whole. What
I offer here must necessarily be a very meager outline
of the rich and full history which Mr. Philbrick's relations to general education constitute.

More and more in our age is increasing the power of
example. It is becoming the general custom to look up
from the task before us to the history of all such tasks,
and to the manifold performance of the same in other
environments. In the history of popular education in
the United States Boston has been before all others the
city set on a hill. The most numerous, and the best, devices for organizing schools and perfecting the methods
of instruction have come from it. Boston itself, between
the years of 1840 and 1860, passed through one of the
most remarkable epochs of educational progress that we
find in history. It threw off the old shell of the ungraded district school system and adopted a new organization better fitted for a city school system.

The student of our educational history will eagerly
search in the records of this city to find the successive
steps that inaugurated this great change. He cannot fail
to observe that the most prominent actor in this change
was John D. Philbrick. The cities and villages of the
mighty Northwest, and, following their lead, the cities
and villages of the Southwest, have been organized upon

the Boston system of the graded school. The idea of this system is in the head of every successful school manager in the new states of this country, and, in most cases, I might add, it is not fully known how great a debt is due to Boston for this idea. Boston is freely and generally accredited with numerous minor ideas relating to school architecture and the courses of study, but only a few know what deep and radical principles of organization have proceeded from this city "set on a hill."

Most teachers who find themselves acting in an organization suppose themselves to be doing what the unenlightened common sense of the individual would dictate. They think that school buildings were always built just as they are now, and schools organized and classes arranged just as they arrange them. They do not realize that every item of architecture, every item of the course of study and method of instruction and management has grown into vogue through fires of opposition ; that they have supplanted other forms of doing these things.

We must not suppose that even the ungraded country school is a rude product of nature and unaided common sense ; even it has a long evolution behind it. But, consider what changes are necessary when you pass from the ungraded school organized by a teacher with his twenty-five pupils in some single room in a district to the large school in the city. In the country, sparsity of population makes unnecessary whole ranges of school culture. The city demands, first of all, that its children shall be taught to live in one community without quarrels ; that, on the other hand, they shall learn to live together in a co-operative spirit. For this it is necessary before all that the children of the city shall be brought together in large schools; instead of twenty or thirty pupils there must be five hundred or a thousand in one school. Hence arises the necessity of inventing wise methods of organization in order to civilize these masses of children and secure humane results.

It appears that, in 1789, at a town meeting in Boston, a report was presented from a committee of honored citizens recommending the establishing of three schools, respectively located in the northern, southern, and central districts of the city. These schools were to belong to what was called for a long time the "double-headed system." They were to have one department called a "writing school," in which was taught writing and arithmetic under one master, and another department called a "reading school," likewise under an independent master, in which was taught reading, spelling, orthoepy, and grammar. The pupils of these schools were to be boys and girls from seven to fourteen years, after they had attended the infant schools, or "women's schools." The boys might attend the year round, but the girls could attend only from April 20th to October 20th. These pupils were to attend the writing school one half of the day, and the reading school the other half of the day. Here is the organization of the system of schools of Boston for more than half a century. Mr. Philbrick was appointed head master of the first single-headed school, — the Quincy School, — Sept. 6th, 1847, before the new building to be named "The Quincy School" was completed. I cannot learn what influence Mr. Philbrick had in determining the plans that were adopted in the new building which he occupied in 1848. I learn only that Dr. T. M. Brewer was chairman of the school, and that great credit is given to Hon. John H. Wilkins, chairman of the Public Building Committee, in conjunction with George B. Emerson, the chairman of the Committee of Conference, appointed by the School Committee. I strongly suspect that to Mr. Emerson was due the radical change in the arrangement of the rooms. Instead of a large study room, with small recitation rooms opening out from it, there were twelve separate rooms intended to be occupied each by a single teacher, who was to have charge of the discipline of the pupils while studying, as well as of the classes when reciting.

This point in regard to architecture is by all means the most important item in the whole plan of organization. Instead of a small room, twenty-eight by thirty-two feet, and holding fifty-six pupils, make a large room holding one hundred and fifty pupils and you change the entire *morale* of the school. While a humane, well-balanced teacher can easily manage the small room and secure excellent discipline with very little or no corporal punishment, it requires a person of strong gifts in the direction of discipline, — so strong, indeed, as to overbalance his other qualities, — to control and discipline the large room. The tendency of the school system with the large room is constantly toward the employment of bullies and tyrants as head masters. The influence of the whole school then goes toward military discipline sustained by brute force. I remember hearing an usher in a Boston school so far back as 1845 boast that the head master whipped up forty rattans in one morning in suppressing a rebellion among his boys. In the St. Louis schools, when I entered them in 1858, where the large-room plan prevailed, it was not uncommon for over one hundred cases of corporal punishment to take place in one day in a school building containing less than five hundred pupils.

The pupils in the small rooms remain under the discipline of the same teacher, both in recitation and in study, and teacher and pupil come to know each other and to feel an intimate sympathy, whereas, in the large room system, the number of pupils prevents intimate acquaintance on the part of the head master, who is responsible for the discipline. The constant danger of demoralization renders summary measures indispensable. Every case of misbehavior attracts the attention of one hundred and fifty pupils. The teacher can have very little power to hold so many pupils in subordination by the influence of his eye and voice. In the small room a case of misbehavior disturbs only fifty pupils, and the teacher easily holds the room under control by a mere look or a mere word. I have not begun to name the advantages of the new building over the old ; but it very soon reduced the cases of corporal punishment to one tenth as many as before, and finally to one-hundredth of the former number. Pupils were humanized ; the teacher's will penetrated each soul intimately and became an unconscious governing power, and, finally, the pupils became self-governed.

In the system of schools of St. Louis after the adoption of the Boston style of building, corporal punishment decreased from an average of five hundred cases per week for seven hundred pupils to three cases for that number. Judge of the benefit to the schools of the Central Plain of the United States from this architectural innovation of Boston. But another benefit of almost equal magnitude arose from the close grading of classes which the new system produced. I think that Mr. Philbrick alone deserves the credit for most of this latter improvement. The large school was graded into classes from the lowest to the highest so as to bring together in each room only those of the same grade of advancement in their studies. According to the ungraded system, such as exists in small country schools now, each teacher had pupils of all grades, from those just beginning to read up to those studying algebra and perhaps Latin. Twenty-five pupils in the country school admit of classification into divisions of two or three pupils at most, and the result is, forty recitations for the day's work, and five or ten minutes to each recitation. It is obvious that no thorough work can be done on this plan ; no searching analysis of the recitation, no discussion of the thought, no experiments to illustrate it, — nothing, nothing but mere committing to memory and repeating the words by rote, — no explanation of the process of an arithmetical problem, but only a memorizing of the rule, and an inspection of the figures in which the answer is stated. The ungraded school in which this method of procedure did not prevail was a rare phenomenon. In the graded school each teacher has two classes, — one recites while the other learns its lesson. The recitation is as long as the attention of the pupil can be held without over-strain, — twenty to twenty-five minutes in the lower grades, and thirty to forty minutes in the highest classes of the grammar school. Time is given for review of the previous lesson, for investigation of the lesson for the day, for discussion of authorities, for illustrations, for hints as to methods of study. Each pupil prepares himself by study of the text-book, and in the recitation sees the subject through the perspective of the minds of his fellow-pupils and teacher, thus widening his own narrow views of the subject by seeing what different aspects it takes on in the minds of his fellow-pupils. He acquires critical alertness by this process and goes to his next lesson with his mind full of new inquiry and reflection, thus re-enforcing his own power of attention by what he has learned from the whole class and the teacher. A good teacher can and does use the recitation as an instrumentality for re-enforcing each individual mind by all the minds of the whole class.

The constant influence, therefore, of the graded school system of Boston has been to change the memoriter system of recitation into a system of critical investigation. Such a system is not possible in an ungraded school, even with a good teacher. Although bad methods are possible with poor teachers, even in a graded system, yet they are no longer necessary, and experience tends to eradicate them altogether.

If we now ask ourselves how it is that, under Mr. Philbrick, the Boston schools attained their world-wide celebrity, we may see two great and sufficient causes in the fact that other parts of the United States have borrowed the system of graded schools from it, and have learned to look upon the Boston schools as the highest achievement in the common school system. Foreign authorities have been quick to perceive this original merit of Boston, and have acknowledged it.

In Boston, more than elsewhere in the country, there have been men of remarkable power and wisdom in the school committee, and, besides these, a very superior class of teachers. The bare fact that Mr. Philbrick held the superintendency for twenty years in such a city would itself imply the strongest eulogium that can be made. He was able to inspire and unite the action of so large a number of men of first-class ability on the school committee. He was able to secure and retain to the last the respect and love of such a corps of teachers. The thing is unprecedented and without the possibility of a parallel elsewhere in our country.

Mr. Philbrick was chosen to organize the graded school system in 1847 on the adoption of the " single-headed " system of organization. All its possibilities were yet to be unfolded. None of them had become apparent. There was no model to go by. Any but a master-mind for organization would have found himself trammeled by the past, and would have failed to develop the advantages of the new, and would thus have retarded the good work. Mr. Philbrick, however, was quick to see what potentialities were in the new, and at once organized them into a

system. An institution once organized carries along
with it, by its own force, a whole system of second-rate
workers, and re-enforces their feeble efforts by the
strength of the organized whole.

As soon as Connecticut had established a normal
school, in 1852, Dr. Henry Barnard, the state superintendent there, secured Mr. Philbrick to organize it. As
principal, he preached in that normal school the new doctrine of graded schools ; and, finally, in institutes all over
the state, held by him after he became the state superintendent, he continued to proclaim the same idea, reaching all the intelligent minds open to new ideas on the
subject of education.

His return to Boston as superintendent, in January,
1857, opened a new epoch. Already the graded system
had been established throughout the city. That was all
done within seven years after the Quincy School had led
the way. Now began his efficient work on the infant
schools. They were classified and organized in accordance with his recommendation, and his untiring supervision of them elevated them to the foremost rank in the
school system for excellence. His wise foresight made
fast this degree of excellence by securing the adoption of
a system of supervision by the grammar school masters,
relieving them from some of the labor of the actual work
of instruction of classes in order to gain the time requisite for this supervision.

To those unacquainted with school supervision, it seems
strange to hear that the mere circumstance of making
the head masters of the schools supervisors over a group

of schools is in itself one of the greatest of school reforms. The routine of school work is very narrowing in
its effects, and continually wears for itself ruts that prevent spontaneity in the teacher. These ruts produce a
degeneration in school work. As soon as the head master begins to have work of supervision over other classes
he begins to recognize new and good methods, and to
carry them from one teacher to the next, thus helping
each by the experience of all. He begins to replace
dead methods by new, live ones, and there begins to be a
vital circulation once more throughout the supervised
school.

I have seen a system of schools adopt gradually the
Boston method of local supervision. I used to say that
the school of four rooms, without supervision, attained a
degree of excellence that could be symbolized by twenty
to forty per cent. ; that is to say, the amount of real
ability brought into actual play in the school was only
twenty to forty per cent. of the possible power of the
teachers.

Again, in a twelve-room school, with a little supervision on the part of the principal teacher, the average
degree of excellence in discipline and instruction arose
to forty or sixty per cent. of the possibility in the teachers. But, in a larger school, when the principal teacher
gave his or her time nearly all to supervising, the average
of actual excellence arose as high as eighty to one hundred per cent. of the capacity. The assistants felt new
powers of work, and lived in a sort of vitalized atmos-
phere, accomplishing what they could never have be-

lieved it possible to accomplish under the system without supervision.

Organized supervision holds fast the ground already gained, and moves on to new achievements, for supervision means that the individual contributions to methods of discipline and instruction are seen by the supervisor and carried to all others, so that each teacher is re-enforced by all, and all by each.

The inventory of the great items of Mr. Philbrick's work as an educator includes, besides the organization of the graded school system, a multitude of suggestions regarding the proper methods of teaching special branches of study. These are to be found scattered through his school reports. The introduction of industrial drawing into the Boston schools, the state law making it obligatory on all cities of 10,000 inhabitants, the importing of the requisite experience and teaching ability from the great English Art School at South Kensington, the establishment of the State Normal Art School, and, finally, the spread of this branch of instruction to all the cities of the land, — Mr. Philbrick receives justly great honor for the very prominent share that he had in this movement, both as an originator and organizer.

To him, also, is due the introduction of evening schools, schools for licensed minors, and the evening high schools.

In the matters of school architecture the questions of hygiene greatly interested him. He discusses the most important advances in this matter over and over in his reports. The size of playgrounds, gymnastics and calisthenics, ventilation, proper heating, and, above all, the proper lighting of schoolrooms, were favorite themes of discussion and suggestion with him. The size of the schoolroom, the method of seating by single desks, the lighting of the room from the left side of the pupil by numerous windows ascending to the ceiling of the room, the proper size of the school for the best purposes of grading and classification, have been discussed by him in a thoughtful manner.

I come to what is, perhaps, his greatest intellectual trait. He believed in the study of the history of peda-gogy. He prided himself on possessing the best library of education to be found in private hands in America. His motto was: "Study education as a whole," — know it as it is at home and abroad. You will find that the history of education contains the career of most educa-tional ideas, showing their inception and adoption, and their subsequent effects, and, if they proved wanting on trial, you will find that also in the history of education.

He had attained that noblest ideal of the supervisor which we have described as exercising the function of taking from each one the original and valuable devices of method, and transplanting the same into the daily work and routine of the others. He now held that the super-visor must take all education, past and present, into his survey, and try to improve his system of schools by intro-ducing the good elements wherever found, and eliminat-ing the bad. "Prove all things and hold fast to that which is good." Of course each teacher has his idio-syncrasy and cannot be helped by all methods that are

good for others. Each is in need of some specific, as it
were ; hence there must be careful and wise study of the
history and laws of growth of one's own system before
one undertakes to modify it in any particular.

Mr. Philbrick's aim was to be judicial, and not parti-
san. This appeared even in his style of writing his
reports. He scarcely completes a sentence advocating a
much needed reform before he hastens to make qualifications suggested by experience and reflection. The
reform is not a cure-all, not a nostrum infallible in all
cases, but is good under such and such conditions. He
proceeds to quote its hostile critics, and to show just
wherein they are right. Almost all the great pedagogical reformers have been men of one idea. Mr. Philbrick
was a many-sided reformer, and held that a reform is
unworthy of its name until it can be reduced to practice.

With his wide glance taking in the entire field of education and cordially recognizing genuine merit everywhere, it was quite natural that he came to be recognized
himself in all quarters of the world. In Spain, Russia,
Japan, Austria, Belgium, England, and Scotland, and
especially in France, he was the best known of American
educators, and all foreign circles were prompt to acknowledge his eminence and show him honor. It was fortunate
for our nation that Massachusetts sent this man to take
charge of its educational exhibit in 1873 at the world exposition at Vienna. It was more fortunate that the Bureau
of Education selected him in 1878 as commissioner in
charge of our national educational exhibit at Paris. He
took in the situation at a glance. Being thoroughly

familiar with the peculiarities of all systems he could come
at once to the special point of interest in our own system which he wished to bring to the attention of the for-
eigner. To this ability is due the fact that Massachusetts
secured a grand diploma of honor at the Vienna Exposition. At Paris, America carried off the lion's share of
honor for its education. It received 121 awards, more
than any other nation except France herself. He secured
for us by his unremitting diligence twenty-eight gold
medals, forty-four silver, and twenty-four bronze medals,
besides twenty-five certificates of honorable mention.
The French Directory distinguished him personally for
his able efforts by creating him a " Chevalier of Honor "
and an " Officer of Public Instruction " (with the insignia
of gold palm and title of " Officer of the Academy "),
while the ancient and venerable University of St. Andrews in Scotland gave him the degree of Doctor of
Laws, " holding in regard," as the Senatus declared, " the
high merits of Mr. Philbrick's work in the sphere of education."

The Belgian Inspector of Schools declared that at
Vienna he learned more from Dr. Philbrick than from
all other sources. The Japanese ministry make a similar strong acknowledgment of his aid to them in planting English schools in Japan. In foreign accounts of
education in the United States, the Boston system always
bears away the palm as the highest type of our national
system of education. In the generous report of M. C.
Hippeau on our education, in the very favorable report
of Bishop Fraser, in the hostile exposition of Rev. James

H. Rigg, and finally in the accurate presentation of our system in Mr. Francis Adams' masterly work on *The Free Schools of the United States*, Boston stands foremost in a rank all by itself.

M. Buisson, French Commissioner to our Philadelphia Exposition, commends in high terms the Boston schools and pays equal honor to Mr. Philbrick. He commends the plans of the Boston school buildings and the civil behavior of the pupils. Mr. Philbrick's school reports were and are eagerly sought for by all directors of educational systems, both here and in Europe. They find an author who discusses questions of education in the full light of existing practice everywhere.

These gratifying tokens of recognition of the subject of our eulogium suggest to us that there is a side to his personal character which has been dwelt on by those who have spoken here to-day before me, that has a national and even international significance. His conciliatory habit of mind, always endeavoring to see both sides of a question and always trying to do justice to opponents, was the basis of a cordial relation that grew up between himself and fellow-educators everywhere in this country and in Europe.

In private life his amiability was charming. He seemed to feel it his duty to encourage young men in the profession by kind words of appreciation wherever he could see any merit. In his official visits to the schools he made the teacher feel that he was a friend and " not a mere task-master trying to spy out defects."

Through his labor on a programme of exercises for the

school he strove to break up the mechanical modes of drill which crept into the system. Inasmuch as education accomplishes its good things by repetition and drill, the best work of the teacher is continually liable to degenerate into lifeless routine. It is true that in habit and routine lies the force of moral education. What are regularity, punctuality, silence, and industry, the four cardinal virtues of school training, but mechanical habits when thoroughly learned, — notwithstanding they lie at the basis all moral training whatsoever. The pupil must learn self-restraint and subjugate his caprice and wilfulness before he can become a thoroughly rational being. How to balance spontaneity and prescription is the constant problem in education, and this Dr. Philbrick knew better than any other man.

It must be acknowledged that the work of the school superintendent is, even at the best, nine tenths of it negative and preventive, to one tenth positive and constructive. He has constant need of vigilance to repress one-sided and injurious efforts, — to hold back even the good teachers, even the good members of the school committee, from extremes. An excellent superintendent appears to outsiders as though he were a mere balance-wheel, or even a dead weight, hindering vital movement and adding no momentum himself.

But the superintendent must see the real healthy, vital movement of the system of schools, and, like a good physician, prevent congestions and inflammations in any of its parts. Occupied in this way for most of his time he can never receive his full meed of appreciation. He will have bitter enemies in the schools and outside of the schools.

Happy, therefore, was Dr. Philbrick in his uncomplaining, unresenting disposition. Even in his last great trial, the gradual shutting down of darkness upon his eyesight, he was never known to complain, and only once indicated the great affliction which his blindness was to him. When he found that his eyesight failed to distinguish the large letters of a new Bible which had been purchased for his daily reading, the tears silently coursed down his cheeks, observed only by his faithful mate, no word indicating his deep sorrow.

His cheerfulness and courage in all emergencies was a perpetual fountain of strength to all his teachers and co-workers in the system of education wherein he performed his life work.

In taking leave of him after this brief and inadequate summary of the events which have made him so widely known and respected by educators at home and abroad, there comes into my mind the words that I love to quote from the prophet Daniel, — the words which are quoted in the epitaph on the tomb of Fichte in Berlin : —

"The teachers shall shine as the brightness of the firmament, and they that turn many to righteousness, as the stars forever and ever."

Reform

of

The Tenure of Office of Teachers.

———•—•———

By John D. Philbrick, LL. D.

Reform of the Tenure of Office of Teachers.

Good teachers, and what next? There is no next. This is the meaning of Jules Simon in his saying, "The master is the school." In this sense the great German pedagogue, when asked what his system was, made the well-known reply, "I am the system." This was Garfield's thought, when paying a merited tribute to his great college-master, he said, "Give me a log hut with only a simple bench, Mark Hopkins on one end and I on the other, and you may have all the buildings, apparatus, and libraries." This was Horace Mann's idea in declaring the teacher's seminary to be one of the greatest instrumentalities for the improvement of the race. Hence, the pivotal question in pedagogy is the question of the teacher, everywhere and always. The cause of education and the cause of the teacher are one. The best criterion of merit in a school system is to be found in the character and qualities of the teachers in its service.

There is no really fruitful educational reform which does not provide for increasing the competence of teachers. The originators and founders of our normal school system, Olmstead, Carter, Russell, Brooks, Mann, Barnard, and others, all maintained and acted upon this theory. They held that the end in view, the ideal education, imparted

in the ideal school, could come only through the ideal
teacher. In maintaining this theory they stood on solid
ground; their position was impregnable. The instrumentality which they advocated as essential for the realization of their idea, was the normal school for the professional training of teachers. Too much cannot be said in
praise of their labors and devotion to this great cause.
The establishment of normal schools was a great achievement. It is not to be doubted that the normal school is
an essential element in a good school system. But history does not justify the assumption that it is the fundamental requisite for securing competent teachers. Something else more fundamental still is necessary to the full
success and the full utilization of the capabilities of the
normal school. That prerequisite is a desirable status
for the teacher who has made his preparation in the normal school.

The creation of such a status has no doubt been too
much overlooked and neglected by our educational leaders
and reformers, and the reason is obvious. The indispensable requisite for such a status is security, — certainty
of position; such security and certainty of position as is
afforded by tenure of office during efficiency and good
behavior. Fifty years ago this reform was impracticable.
Every school system must, in the nature of things, be in
substantial harmony with the other institutions of the
country where it exists. In forming the school system
of France, Guizot and Cousin took lessons of Prussia and
Holland, but they were obliged to adapt their plan to
the actual state of things in their own country.

Mr. Forster, on drawing up his school bill, the new Magna Charta of the English people, had at his command all the available results of foreign experience ; but he was under the necessity of shaping every provision with' reference to existing national institutions and customs. So our educational pioneers of half a century ago had to shape the fabric and spirit of our school system, so far as they were instrumental in introducing modifications and improvements, in conformity with existing political and social arrangements. Hence any attempt on their part to advocate any reform relating to the status of the teacher, in conflict with the prevailing theory and practice touching the status of other public servants, would have been impracticable and utterly futile. Improvements do not advance on all lines simultaneously. They made advancement where advancement was possible.

Now what was the status of public officers and employes, whether in the service of the Nation, the State, or the municipality, fifty years ago, in respect to tenure of office ? Our political institutions are founded upon the theory that public officers are public servants, and precisely at that period, more than at any time in our history, the opinion prevailed that the officers and employes of the public had no interest or property whatever in the offices and situations which they occupied. Out of this prevailing sentiment grew the pernicious custom of what is called rotation in office ; where the tenure of office was not fixed by law, as in the case of the Judiciary, custom limited the tenure to one or two years. Taking advantage of the prevalence of this sentiment, which claimed for itself the credit of being the spirit of true democracy, President Jackson inaugurated the custom of removing officers without regard to their qualifications for their duties or their behavior.

The assumption and exercise of this arbitrary authority made the public officers in the service of the Nation dependent for their bread and butter on the will of the executive. Nearly all State officers, from the governor down, held their office, for the most part, for a single year only ; the same was the case with municipal officers, including school committee. In some States even the judges of the highest court were elected by the people, to hold office for a short determinate period ; and so the office of teacher of public schools, which, in the days of Master Cheever, was held by life tenure, was made to conform to the general custom in respect to tenure of office ; and even the clergy, who had always held by life tenure, began to hold by a limited tenure. He, therefore, must have been not only a bold man, but an unwise one, who, as an educational reformer, should have in those days dreamed of undertaking to render the status of the teacher more desirable by advocating for him a permanent tenure of office. Hence the reformers of those days directed their efforts to other objects.

But an immense change has taken place since that time in public opinion, as well as in legislative provision, respecting the tenure of office of public officials. The civil service reform, to which has been accorded the largest plank in the platform of the dominant political party, is a declaration of the principle that *Justice to servants is essential to good service*, and that justice is incompatible with the tenure of office, which carries with it no ownership or interest on the part of the incumbent.

The essence of the civil service reform consists in its aim to substitute a permanent tenure of office for the short and uncertain tenure ; all the rest is incidental. This carries with it appointments and promotions by merit, and not by favoritism. This revolution in public sentiment has made the opportunity to undertake a reform in the status of the teacher by making his tenure of office permanent. To secure a permanent tenure of office for teachers in the public schools is the next great step to be taken in the interest of the people's schools. In my judgment this is the most important educational reform of our school system that has ever been undertaken. The substitution of the permanent tenure for the present precarious limited tenure would doubtless be regarded by teachers as a great boon, but I am looking more especially to the public welfare, — the public interest is the paramount interest.

The theory which it is my present purpose to propound and advocate is this : Permanency of tenure would enormously increase the desirableness of the teacher's status ; that while it costs nothing to the public to grant this permanency, to the teachers it would be an inestimable boon ; that, as a means of compensating teachers, it would be equivalent to a vast increase of school revenue ; that the salary, even though raised to the highest practicable limit, when subject to the offset of short and

precarious tenure, with all its train of evils, is insufficient
to bring into the service of teaching, and retain there the
requisite teaching talent.   In substance, then, the question of permanent tenure for teachers is, in the first
place, a question of economy, — the question of conser-
vation of forces ; that is, the question whether the money
compensation of teachers shall be in effect largely sup-
plemented by what costs nothing.   In the second place,
it is a question of educational results, — for salary plus
permanent tenure is the indispensable condition of the
ideal teaching corps, and hence the indispensable condition of the ideal school and the ideal education.

The reasoning on which this theory is based is extremely simple, and is the following :

1. Permanancy of situation everywhere and always
counts largely with the salary in estimating the emolu-
ment of the situation, and it is self-evident that these
two elements together are greater than one of them
alone.

2. The addition of permanency of tenure to salary is
necessary to make teaching a career sufficiently attractive
for persons of ability and culture, as a life work, and it
is only from such persons devoted to teaching as a life
work that the best teaching can come.

This reasoning is the plain lesson of history, which he
who runs may read.   It is well known that the German
States, and more especially Prussia, took the lead in the
organization and development of the modern system of
public instruction.   And it appears that in Prussia from
the outset the life tenure of office for the teachers was

adopted as the first principle of the incipient system; and, in fact, the Prussian law long ago expressly prohibited the appointment of any regular teacher for a determinate period. This was the original stock upon which improvements were from time to time grafted, until at length its present vigor, completeness, and symmetry of development have been produced. Forty years ago Horace Mann thus characterized the teachers produced by this system: "As a body of men their character is more enviable than that of any of the three so-called 'professions.'" In all the other European countries the point of departure and the process of development have been substantially the same. It is safe, I think, to say that in no one of them has it been thought expedient to attempt to carry on a system of schools on the plan of choosing teachers for a short, determinate period.

On the other hand, it seems to have everywhere been taken for granted that there could not be such a thing as an efficient and economical school system without making provision for securing the services of teachers who should be devoted to the business of instruction as a life profession. Accordingly, we find that, although public school teachers have, perhaps, nowhere received entirely satisfactory treatment, they have generally been secure in their position and in their revenues, all too slender though they may have been. Thus the beginning was made by laying a foundation for a status of dignity and independence. This was all important as the initial provision. The rest followed logically, although not without delays and difficulties. As it is the teacher that gives

character to the school, which no well-informed person
will deny, so we find that most of the measures of progress and improvement have been such as were calculated
to ameliorate the condition and elevate the status of the
teacher, to provide better professional training, to improve the scheme of examination and certificating of candidates, to increase the compensation, to secure a more
competent and trustworthy superintendence and inspection, to afford the best means of appreciating and rewarding merit.   These were the objects always uppermost in
the aims and efforts of intelligent promoters of educational progress.   And thus by degress have been created
the conditions requisite to render teaching a veritable
career ; not a career, indeed, leading to wealth and lux-
ury, but a career of assured independence, dignity, and
support.

In our country the point of departure and the process
of development have been quite different from those we
have considered.   We have undertaken to develop and
build up an efficient system of instruction while acting
on the assumption that the teacher cannot be recognized
as having a claim to any ownership in a position of
service.

In a French report on English schools it is stated as a
curious absurdity, that at the annual meeting of the
trustees of a certain old endowed school in London, the
headmaster is summoned into their presence, and informed that the term of his service is at an end and the
mastership vacant.   Thereupon, if he desires to be considered a candidate for reëlection he so states, and retires

and waits for the result of the ballot. This is a type of the tenure of office of substantially all American public school teachers. Their position is not assured beyond the term of one year. Nor is this the worst condition of their tenure; there is a lower deep yet. In general, the public school teacher may be dismissed within the year for which he is elected by a majority of the school board, the teacher so dismissed having no legal right to a previous notice, a hearing, or appeal to a superior authority. This is the tenure in Massachusetts, and so far as I have been able to ascertain, it is substantially the same in other states.

Mr. Boutwell, in speaking of this in his commentary on the Massachusetts school law, justly remarks, "This power is as nearly absolute as any power in our government." In point of law, therefore, the American public school teacher holds office securely not even for the short period of one year. His position, salary, and professional standing are absolutely at the mercy of the local committee. A majority of a quorum of the school board, by a secret ballot, may dismiss him without a day's notice, without bringing any charge against him, and the dismissal so made is absolute and final. This tenure may have some slight safeguards in some states, or some individual cities; if so, let them be known and credited therefor. The only exception within my knowledge worthy of mention is that of the city of New York, where the tenure is permanent, removals being made only for cause. It has been ascertained that in the cities of Brooklyn, Jersey City, and Newark, the tenure is also

during efficiency and good behavior. In our system,
therefore there has been provided as yet no solid foundation upon which to build up a desirable status for the
teacher ; consequently little has been done to environ the
teacher's office with the subsidiary guarantees requisite
to constitute a career of teaching service. The condition
of absolute insecurity and dependence in respect to position is necessarily compensated in some degree by the
rate of the salary. In fact, our system, instead of taking
permanency of tenure as the point of departure from
which to develop a competent teaching corps in accordance with the opinion and practice prevailing in all other
enlightened countries, has relied primarily and mainly
upon compensation in money as the mainspring in the
scheme for securing the desired teaching service.

This peculiarly and distinctively American feature of
public instruction is coeval with the modern organization
of our school system. It has been on trial for a long
time, on an extensive scale and with all sorts of conditions. It is time now to ask, What has been the outcome
of this experiment? In reply to this question it may be
said, without contradiction, that the American plan of
dealing with teachers has not built up a stable and permanent profession of teaching.

The failure of our system of instruction to secure the
services of a body of teachers devoted for life to the work
was set forth in the remarkable Report on American
Education by the French Commission, of which the eminent educator, M. Buisson, was the president, and con-
trasted with the success in this respect of the French

system. "In France," says the reporter,* "one embraces the career of teaching with the intention of creating for himself a stable and permanent position. Those who abandon it before having obtained their retiring pension form the exception. The young beginner expects to live and die a teacher; and each year of exercise adding to the experience previously acquired, a moment arrives when, possessing a competency of knowledge, both theoretical and practical, he can conduct his school with method, with success, and thus limit the *rôle* of his superiors to simple encouragement and kindly advice. In the United States it is otherwise. The profession of a teacher would appear to be a sort of stage, where the girl waits for an establishment suited to her taste, and the young man a more lucrative position. For many young persons this temporary profession is the means of procuring the funds to continue their studies. Few masters count more than four or five years of service, and if instructresses remain longer in the profession it must be remembered that marriage is ordinarily the end of their desires ; and that once married, they almost always withdraw from the service."

If this is the correct statement of the case, and that it is, I think will be generally agreed, then our system has failed to create a stable, permanent profession of teaching ; while such a profession has been created not only by the French system, but by the systems of all other enlightened countries except our own. My inference is

*Monsieur B. Berger, Inspector General and Director of National Pedagogical Museum.

that the failure of our system in this vital particular is owing to the short and precarious tenure of office of the teacher. No argument is needed to prove that, other things being equal, teaching as a career, as a life-work, yields vastly better results than teaching as a temporary occupation.

I would not be understood, however, to admit for a moment that our system of free schools, as a whole, has been a failure ; on the contrary, it has been a great success, whatever may be said in its disparagement from ignorance or bad intent. The last thought given to the world by Barnas Sears, than whom no higher authority on the subject can be cited, bore on this point, and was expressed in the following words : " If the old district school in New England, imperfect as it was, bore good fruit, which none deny, the modern system, with its manifold improvements, has borne them much more abundantly ; and yet we have not reached the goal for which we are striving." This is the testimony of a wise and true reformer, ripe in wisdom and experience, who recognized and defended acquisitions already won while earnestly striving for still further advancement.

The goal for which we are all confessedly striving is the most economical and efficient system of instruction, and the history of education proves that the best results in instruction are produced only where teaching is pursued as a career for life ; and second, it teaches also that permanency of tenure is essential as a means of rendering teaching a desirable career.

To render the permanent tenure effectual it must be

accompanied by a permanent, that is, an irreducible salary, as control of salary is virtually control of tenure.

We know what the objector to this plan will say : Your permanent tenure, with its irreducible salary, constitutes without doubt a desirable status for the teacher, providing the rate of salary is not too low. Whatever other tribulations may await the teacher, he has no longer any risks to run ; he has no longer to submit to an annual humiliation in the shape of an annual election ; his reputation and his living are no longer at the mercy of incompetent and prejudiced school officers. His status is invested with dignity and independence ; he can hold up his head like a man, and look the whole world in the face. But in all this what have we done but shift the risk from the employe to the employer, from the teacher to the public ; you have insured the teacher against risk, but what guaranty has the public that the teacher will do his duty when he has no longer the fear of losing his situation, to act as a spurr to effort. Are not the annual election and the power of summary dismissal necessary means of stimulating teachers to vigorous and sustained effort, and of removing those who are delinquent and incompetent ; and, besides, is not this permanency of tenure contrary to the spirit of our free institutions, and too un-American to find favor with us ?

To this question, which embodies the substance of all that can be said in favor of annual election, and the power of summary dismissal, I reply : First, that the precarious tenure has not been found necessary for the end in view in any other enlightened country on the globe ;

and, second, in our own country, the annual election is unknown in universities, colleges, and the higher educational institutions, generally, outside of the public school system, so that this odious annual election has no place in the civilized world except the public schools of the United States. But we do not deny that the public should be guaranteed against risk as well as the teacher. In the adjustment of compensation and service the relation of risks must always be taken into account. In this case the guaranty of the public against risk is perfectly feasible, as experience has satisfactorily proved. This guaranty consists of six distinct provisions:

1. A thorough professional training of teachers in normal schools suited to their destined functions. This is necessary as the primary guaranty against the appointment of teachers without the requisite qualifications. And it is evident that the state could afford a more liberal expenditure for the education of a teacher who is to serve the public thirty or forty years than for the teacher who is to serve only three or four years. Only a small fraction of the teachers now engaged in the service are graduates of normal schools, there being no one state that has not recoiled before the task of securing to the whole body of teachers a professional education, and this is because of the very great number of teachers which teaching as a temporary employment necessitates.

2. Another guaranty should be provided by a system of examining and certificating teachers by experts wholly under the control of the central authorities; and, besides, the local certificate, the only one, with few exceptions,

now issued, does little for the establishment of the standing and reputation of the holder. But a certificate granted by the central authority, and valid throughout the state, would create a professional rank and standing which would elevate the status of the holders.*

3. As a third condition requisite to the permanent tenure, probationary service must be provided. The candidate must not only have his certificate, but he must prove his capacity by actual service in teaching, before he can claim a definitive appointment. The period of probation should not be less than two years, and it might well be three or four. The judgment on the result should be rendered by one or more approved experts. If a further guaranty against failure is deemed expedient, it may be obtained by an examination at the end of the probation, bearing especially on the practical work of ·the schoolroom.

4. As to the choice to be made among candidates thus prepared, the most judicious method appears to be for the superior school authority to nominate three or four candidates, having regard both to seniority and merit, and that the election from this list should be left to the local committee.

5. Provision for a suitable hierarchical situation for the teacher. Such a situation would comprise a competent supervision and the other means requisite for stimulating the teacher to the best efforts, by recognizing his worth and rewarding his merits ; and such a situation would also comprise the necessary machinery for administering

* Provision has been made for state certificates in a few of the states.

just and salutary discipline in cases of delinquency. In France the hierarchical situation is so well contrived that the young man of talents, entering upon his career as primary teacher in the remotest mountain hamlet, may hope to reach, by well-earned promotions, the principalship of a metropolitan school, or to become director of a normal school, or even inspector.

"It is the function of a good administration," says the eminent Belgian publicist and educator, De Laveleye, "to seek by fixed rules which science indicates to ascertain merit, and to class individuals according to their aptitudes; then there would be an end of solicitations, of subserviency, of intrigues, of protections, of favors, of injustices." And this is the paradise for which the teacher prays. He wants to feel that he owes his position to his merit, and not to favor, and to be sure that his efforts will be appreciated and recompensed. It is perhaps, in vain to hope that the public school teacher's path may be strewn with roses, but hitherto it has been too much hedged up with briers and thorns; but the supreme misery of his lot is to be judged by incompetents. This would necessarily be mitigated by the better supervision which the permanent tenure would require.

6. A retiring pension is requisite, not only as a security for old age, but as a means of rendering practicable the retirement of the aged and fatigued public servant, without reflecting on his reputation or abandoning him to destitution.

These six conditions are logically involved in the full and complete application of the principle of fixity of tenure. Moreover, they are at the same time the means of producing an equilibrium of risks and of authorities, which experience has proved to be indispensable to the most efficient, economical, and harmonious working of a school system.

In every point of view this reform in our system seems to me fundamental in its importance; all others are but secondary, subordinate, accessory. It may seem to the timid to be a bold undertaking, but it is not more bold in the present circumstances than was the project of state normal schools, or the project of a state board of education fifty years ago. Every epoch has its peculiar task. This reform I verily believe to be the task of the hour for the friends of educational progress. Public sentiment is now everywhere drifting in this direction. In the powerful movement which has been begun to reform the civil service, I plainly see the dawning of a new and better day for the public school and the public school teacher. The press is daily teeming with arguments for our cause, for the principles of a good civil service are essentially the same as the principles of a good educational service. Hence the achievement of the civil service reform will prepare the way for this reform. The spoils system and the annual election are twin barbarisms, and with the abolition of the former the latter must go.

But permanent tenure is not to be brought into successful operation by a single legislative act. This radical reform must be reached by a series of steps. Initiatory steps have already been taken in various quarters.

It is worthy of mention that, at the late session of the Massachusetts Legislature, the chairman of the Committee on Public Service offered to include the teaching service in the provision of the civil service reform bill reported by his committee. This reform must begin practically in the cities and larger towns. Teachers have their duty in connection with this task. Everywhere they should pour in their petitions and memorials upon the legislatures, throughout the country, and do their share of the work in creating public opinion which shall demand this reform.

Last - Days

and

Funeral Rites.

Last Days and Funeral Rites.

LAST DAYS.

Dr. Philbrick's last sickness probably dates back to the spring of 1882, when he made a journey to the far West. This journey involved some long and tedious rides, which, with the- labor of visiting schools, were too great a tax upon his strength. In June, after his return home, he was so ill as to call his family physician, Dr. Carlton. For two months, July and August, he was confined to the house, in which time he read much, and often in bed. In October he seemed to take a severe cold, which so affected his eyes that they were sore and painful. In time, as the result of some simple remedies, they became comparatively well, but, when the cold winds of winter set in, they again became very painful, so much so that Dr. Carlton wished an oculist to see them.

Accordingly, Dr. Coggin of Salem was called to see him in January, 1883. He pronounced the disease a severe rheumatic affection, but he also saw indications of what his friends had already feared, namely, a loss of sight. This Dr. Philbrick had himself feared from the very first, as an inherited trouble, because several of his relatives on his mother's side had been totally blind.

In January, 1884, Drs. Coggin and Carlton performed an operation upon one eye, hoping to let more light into it, but the operation was not a success, and so the experiment was not repeated upon the other eye. From this time on his sight became more and more impaired. Still he was able to move about his own house with comparative ease ; but, when in a strange place, he moved so much more cautiously that he seemed to see much less than at home.

In the spring of 1884 he began his work on City School Systems in the United States. His devoted wife read to, and wrote for him. So constantly did he work that, by the end of August, he had the work more than half written. At that time he employed an amanuensis, Miss Dudley, a relative of his, who spent a year with him. She was a graduate of the Salem Normal School, and was thus pretty well prepared for the work required of her. During the year which Miss Dudley read and wrote for him, he finished his work on City Systems, and wrote the paper on School Reports, which is printed in the *Proceedings of the Council of Education* for 1885 ; he also did a great amount of preparatory reading, making notes, etc., for a work on State Systems, which he hoped to write in the winter of 1885-6. It was in the summer of 1884 that he gave the address before the American Institute on "Reform of Tenure of Office of Teachers."

In the summer of 1885 he, in company with Mrs. Philbrick, went to Hanover, where he served on the examining committee of the college ; then to Newport to the meeting of the American Institute, then to Saratoga to attend the meetings of the Council of Education. All these meetings he enjoyed very much, especially those at Saratoga, where he met so many western friends. In September of the same year he visited his old home in Deerfield. It seems not unlikely that all the work of this summer was too much for his impaired strength, for the first severely cold weather in December seemed to affect him unfavorably, so much so that he said he "could not think well."

There were several times during the last year of his life when he could not speak the word he wished to use when talking, and twice he lost entirely the power of speech for an instant. This he felt to be "an indication of something serious," a premonition of what came at last and caused his death. He once spoke to his doctor of it, though, in talking of it, he called it a trouble of the heart; so it would seem doubtful whether he felt clear in his own mind what the real nature of the trouble was.

The weather of the week preceding his fatal attack was very cold, so that he gave up his ride which he was accustomed to take almost every day; this was through fear of bringing on pain in his eyes. Up to Saturday, the 16th of January, 1885, he had hoped he should be able to go to Boston the next week to attend the Quincy School reunion, but that day he said if it continued so cold he could not go. On Sunday he did not seem as well as usual. He complained of headache, so much so that his wife did not leave him to attend church. When Monday morning came he said he did not feel like getting up, but must dictate some letters, one especially to the Quincy School boys. His wife advised him to wait till afternoon, hoping he might get some sleep and feel better. He took his dinner in bed and then dictated three letters.

It was then so late that Mrs. Philbrick feared the amanuensis would not have time to copy them before the mail would leave, and stepped down into the library to help her. When she went back to him, he said, "It has come ; something is the matter with my arm." His wife, thinking it might be numbness, rubbed his arm, but he evidently thought differently. She gave him some hot drinks, hoping to start the circulation more freely, and he soon seemed to feel better. When tea-time came he took a cup of tea and a bit of toast. Mrs. Philbrick then went down to supper, and upon her return inquired how he felt, but he could not readily answer, and she became alarmed and summoned the nearest physician.

This was on Monday evening, Jan. 18, 1886. Dr. Philbrick gradually sank, and died the second day of February following.

Thus ended a noble life. Never was the true nobility of his nature more clearly manifested than during those years of approaching darkness. It was the good fortune of the writer to visit him often in his home during that time, and he never failed to be impressed with the sweetness of his nature and the cheerful Christian resignation with which he bore his great misfortune. Indeed, from anything in the tone of his conversation, no one could ever mistrust that he thought approaching blindness anything more than a part of the experience that was appointed for him by a kind Father. Then with what kindness and broad charity he always spoke of his former co-workers ! He seemed delighted to remember all the good and noble deeds and all the generous words which he had known of others, but to consign differences to oblivion. Many a silent blessing and inspiration has been carried from that noble, patient presence. He still lives in word and deed.

THE FUNERAL SERVICES.

The funeral of Dr. Philbrick was at his home in Danvers, Feb. 4. The public schools of Boston were closed for the day as a token of respect to his memory. The day was one of the coldest and most uncomfortable of the season, and yet a large number of friends from Boston attended the services. Among them were the superintendent of schools, several members of the Board of Supervisors, a large number of the principals, and several former members of the School Committee who had served with Mr. Philbrick. In addition to these, many teachers from other towns, many business men, and a large number of neighbors and friends from Danvers were in attendance, so that the house was crowded with those desirous of honoring the distinguished dead.

The Boston masters showed their old-time love by taking with them a beautiful floral tribute in the form of a closed book, on the cover of which was a crescent of roses and lilies, and within the crescent the word

CLOSED made of carnations. The casket was placed in the parlor beneath a fine oil portrait of the deceased. The portrait was entwined with smilax. The tribute of the Boston masters was placed at the foot of the casket.

The services were conducted by Rev. Charles B. Rice, of Danvers, Mr. Philbrick's pastor. He read from the Scriptures the solemn sentences for the dead, beginning with the passage, " Lord, Thou hast been our dwelling place in all generations," and following with the twenty-third Psalm, and with other selections setting forth the Christian hope concerning the resurrection of the dead and the life to come. He made, also, a brief address, reviewing such portions of Mr. Philbrick's life as had come under his own observation, and touching upon the singular value of the services he had rendered to the public.

ADDRESS OF REV. CHARLES B. RICE.

Mr. Philbrick's chosen work has all been in the line of the elevation of mankind. It has been, throughout, a work of enlightenment, and instruction, and guidance for men. It was work of a higher order than that by which many persons gain for themselves distinction. Now that it is ended, his friends may review it with ample satisfaction and with gratitude.

His life was in many ways representative, also, of the best things in New England. There hangs upon the wall a picture of his early home, — the house in which he was born, — a typical New England farmhouse. From such homes have come many of the men who have been most conspicuous in the world, and whose lives have

most adorned and enriched the land. Mr. Philbrick himself had always a love for the place of his nativity, and
for all the places associated with the events of his domestic life. He cherished this sentiment with respect to
this spot and the house within which these funeral ob-
servances are held. Near at hand is the schoolhouse in
which one of his first schools was taught. Still nearer
stands the ancient house in which he found the lady who
became his wife. It was characteristic, therefore, and
fitting with him, that he should retire to spend here his
closing years. The people of the neighborhood and
town have taken great interest and satisfaction in his
dwelling among them. He was himself, to a rare degree,
a man of genial feelings and kindly sympathies. He
entered easily into the thoughts of children. He was
marked as much by gentleness as by breadth of mind.
His calls at the parsonage, — one of which he made on
the last day of his going abroad for such a purpose,—are
remembered with interest by all the household.

Mr. Philbrick had a wonderful enthusiasm and courage
with respect to his work, holding on upon it in the face
of serious and increasing bodily infirmities. His mental
force was in these last years in no wise abated, and his
literary ability was scarcely at all relaxed. He left off
his labors only with his life.

There is need at such a time of the consolations and
hopes of the Christian faith, since the end of every life,
even the most successful and honorable, must be sad, if,
indeed, all life ended with the present time. Mr. Philbrick was a member, from his youth, of a Christian

church, a daily reader of the Bible, accustomed to recognize the hand of God in the disposings of human affairs and the orderings of nature, and a man having the deepest currents of his life devout, and reverent, and trustful.

ADDRESS OF REV. DR. SPAULDING.

It was my privilege to have formed an acquaintance with Mr. Philbrick at the outset of his college course. He was a member of a large class of nearly one hundred; yet of that number he was individualized by the same characteristics which would be recognized by those who knew him only in his subsequent profession and career. In this way his character, and the life flowing out of that mind and character, seem a unit. It is the same stream, only becoming broader and fuller with the added work of years.

No man in college was more noted than Mr. Philbrick for indefatigable industry. He was not a man of brilliant parts, but he was a man of steady aim, of strong motive power, of inflexible perseverance, so that he was certain to accomplish, and to accomplish well, whatever he might undertake. It was equally certain that he would never propose to himself any common result, yet his was not a vaulting ambition, but a strong, mature, solid purpose. It was thus with his college studies. In the second year of his college course, when the students were called upon to volunteer to take up the study of the differential and integral calculus, Mr. Philbrick was one of the first to go into it. The writer said to him, "John,

what can you find in that which will be of any use?
What can you do with it?" Mr. Philbrick replied,
"There is nothing that I can learn in this world that I
cannot make use of somewhere and somehow." And
this high standard of the value of knowledge he showed
always, from first to last.

His was not an allegiance to mere matters of intellect.
He was a man of the strictest integrity, — a man of high
moral principles in all the conduct of his life. He was
as true to his convictions as the sun in its course. Mr.
Philbrick always stood for what he deemed right, and,
standing there, he never could be moved ; he was a wall
of strength. To the younger members of his class, who
at one time embraced views opposed to what he believed
true, he proved a great help ; opposed to them in opinion, he labored so kindly, so faithfully, with a devotion
so unyielding, that he led them to a deliberation upon the
matter, and brought them to a thorough change of view.

The same sterling firmness of character was seen in
his connection with the public schools of Boston. He
had early decided to give his life to education. This
choice of a profession dated as far back as his sophomore
year, and he had great affection and loyalty to it as a
profession, feeling that it demanded and rewarded all a
man's best powers. His theories were never abstract
views, but matters of vital interest and practical importance, and as such he grappled them "with hooks of
steel." We know how true he was to his convictions in
educational decisions. He would rather suffer personal
defeat than give them up, and he did endure defeat

many times; but he persisted in what he thought right
until his point was gained. Even in circumstances of
great excitement, when he was most earnest for measures, he was remarkably free from any bitter, unkind, or
ungenerous judgments of those who differed from him in
opinion.

Both teachers and pupils could rely on his kindly sympathy; he loved their work. No one could ask aid of
him without feeling that he rejoiced to be a friend and a
helper; he sympathized with the difficulties of another
by bending all his enthusiasm, all his energy, to overcome them.

Mr. Philbrick's wonderful power of discipline was the
natural outgrowth of the order, perseverance, and desire
for progress seen in his early school life. When he came
to regulate schools he knew all about them. When he
was sent to Paris to arrange the educational department
of the United States, it was evident that the government
had put the right man in the right place. He did
remarkable work as an organizer. Nothing was overlooked or neglected; thoroughness of detail stood side
by side with the great principle, "the greatest good of
the greatest number." As a friend of the public schools
no man has done more for their highest and best interests. No words of eulogy are needed for him whose
work has been to mould, to stimulate, and to elevate the
minds of the youth of his time, and to place the results
of the educational system of his country on a broad and
permanent basis in the world's record. For ourselves, it
is well that we should stop to look carefully at such a

work, to take fresh inspiration from so noble a life as that of John D. Philbrick.

ADDRESS OF DANIEL B. HAGAR, Ph. D.

Nearly forty years ago I made my first visit to the Quincy School, in Boston, which was then under the charge of him over whose death we are now called to mourn. I had learned that the school was one of extraordinary excellence. , I found it to be well worthy of its high reputation. Although a stranger to the master, he received me with that genuine courtesy which was one of his marked characteristics. From that day to the close of his life it was my great privilege to regard him as my warm and faithful friend. Coming to know him intimately, I found him in all respects worthy of esteem and confidence. His admirable personal qualities and his intellectual ability attracted to him hosts of friends, and commanded the highest respect of all who best knew him. To young teachers he was always kind, endearing himself to them by the interest he manifested in their welfare and the readiness with which he rendered aid in their behalf.

Mr. Philbrick's work as an educator was too broad and comprehensive to admit of even an outline at the present time. His career was one of vast usefulness. His reputation as a leader in educational affairs is world-wide. Prof. L. W. Mason, while visiting all parts of Europe, investigating methods in his department of instruction, was everywhere greeted with kindly inquiries in regard to Dr. Philbrick, and listened to the warmest expressions of regard for him and his work. The Japanese Minister at Washington states that when commissioners of Japan had been appointed to examine systems of education, with reference to the adoption of the best system for Japan, they visited the principal cities of the United States, including Boston ; they carefully studied the leading systems of Europe, and then returned to Boston, having decided that the Boston system, as devised and conducted by Superintendent Philbrick, was, in their judgment, the best. On their return to Japan, they took with them specimens of the school furniture and the various school appliances of Boston. To-day there may be found in Tokio a Boston schoolroom in all its completeness. As a result of Mr. Philbrick's labors, Boston has long been a Mecca for educators from all parts of the civilized world.

His influence does not end with his life. His wise opinions on educational subjects have been embodied in a series of reports whose excellence has never been surpassed, if ever equaled. Even after he had lost his eyesight, so that he was compelled to write by dictation, he prepared for the National Bureau of Education a report on the city schools of the United States, whose great value cannot be overestimated.

Mr. Philbrick held positive opinions on education, which he maintained with unflinching fidelity, — opinions which were not formed hastily, but were the outcome of extensive knowledge and careful deliberation.

As an educator he may well serve as a model for young men who are ambitious to become distinguished in the field of labor in which he wrought so long and so successfully. His life was one of constant usefulness. We who are teachers mourn over him as a departed friend. Death has come; but to him "death is the crown of life."

ADDRESS OF LARKIN DUNTON, LL. D.

A great and good man has gone to his rest. We meet to-day to pay our last sad tribute of respect to his memory. To know him was to trust him and to love him.

Of all the men of the present generation who have devoted their lives to the cause of popular education, John D. Philbrick was the foremost. I think it not too much to say that among the educational men of all the civilized nations of the world there is not a living man to-day whose name is so widely and so favorably known. Not to know him is to be ignorant of the history of public education.

His profound and minute knowledge of the origin and development of the public school system of Boston is well known to many of those present; but his acquaintance with the school systems of other important cities in this country, and, indeed, with the school systems of all civilized nations, was just as profound and little less minute. I have often heard him say that the best data for determining the value of educational theories and methods were the tendencies of educational practice among civilized nations, and judged by this standard no man was more competent.

I remember well his first official visit to my school. I

was then a subordinate teacher in a grammar school of Boston, where he was superintendent. After listening for half an hour to the school exercises, he drew me into general conversation upon schools, and in a few moments I believed myself in the presence of the wisest school man that I had ever known. This belief has been gaining strength for the last eighteen years. It was my privilege to spend a day with him about a month ago in this very room. He was then in pretty good health and in excellent spirits. I never left him with so profound a sense of his great educational wisdom as on that evening.

Another of his characteristics was his patience. I have never known a man who better understood the value of waiting. He was wonderfully tolerant of opinions at variance with his own, and was quite willing to wait till knowledge and reason had produced conviction.

His mantle of charity was so broad that it covered friends and foes alike. For those who differed from him on matters of educational policy, and even for those who had caused him infinite labor and trouble, he was ever willing to accord the best of motives. He was preëminently a man of sweetness of temper.

Add to this a serene and cheerful mind, a broad, correct judgment, and a keen insight into the tendencies of educational movements, and you have the elements of character that made him so universally respected, trusted, and loved by the old Boston masters with whom he worked for so many years.

To his stricken widow and other mourning relatives, permit me to say, that it has fallen to the lot of few mortals to be so widely known, so highly respected, and so deeply loved.

At the close of these addresses, Mr. Rice read the following letters :

LETTER FROM JOHN G. WHITTIER.

OAK RIDGE, 2d Mo., 4, 1886.

Dear Mrs. Philbrick :—It is not possible for me to be present at the last services to thy honored husband and my very highly esteemed friend and neighbor. I had hoped, not without reason, that he would outlive me, and that we should after have the pleasure of meeting each other in the future. He leaves a noble record, and his memory will long be cherished as a wise and successful friend of learning, and as a worthy and upright citizen.

With sincere sympathy, I am thy friend,

JOHN G. WHITTIER.

LETTER FROM GEN. JOHN EATON.

MARIETTA, O., Feb. 3, 1886.

Mrs. Dr. Philbrick : — Deeply regretting the impossibility of my attending Dr. Philbrick's funeral, I am one of that great number who mourn his death as his personal loss, and whose tenderest sympathies are with you. An able, scholarly, noble man, dear friend, great educator, full of knowledge, wise to plan and faithful to execute, his death is a calamity to sound learning the world over.　　JOHN EATON.

The hymn of Addison, " The Spacious Firmament on High," which Mr. Philbrick learned when a boy, and which was always a favorite with him, and which he repeated during his last sickness, was read, and the excrcises closed with prayer and the benediction. The remains were then placed in the receiving tomb to await final burial in the spring.

THE FINAL INTERMENT.

The remains were removed from Danvers, Mass., the final interment taking place at Deerfield, N. H., May 3, 1886. It was the wish of his neighbors and townsmen that, on this occasion, there should be some simple public services by which they could testify their love and respect to their honored friend. This was arranged for, and on a beautiful spring day, amid a crowded gathering of his early friends at his old homestead, his body was borne to its last rest by the arms of those who had been his pupils nearly fifty years before. Rev. Mr. Walker offered prayer at the house, and Rev. Mr. Kingsbury invoked a blessing at the grave. The following readings and address were given by his friend, Gilman H. Tucker.

READINGS.

"They that put their trust in the Lord are as Mount Zion, that cannot be moved, but abideth forever."

"Man that is born of woman is of few days and full of trouble. He cometh forth like a flower and is cut down; he fleeth also as a shadow and continueth not."

"Let not your heart be troubled : ye believe in God, believe also in me. In my Father's house are many mansions : if it were not so I would have told you. I go to prepare a place for you, and if I go and prepare a place for you I will come again and receive you unto myself, that where I am there ye may be also."

"Eye hath not seen nor ear heard, nor the heart of man conceived the things which God hath prepared for them that love him."

"And I heard a great voice out of Heaven saying, behold the tabernacle of God is with man; and he will dwell with them, and they shall be his people, and God himself shall be with them and be their God."

"I heard a voice from Heaven saying unto me, Write, from henceforth blessed are the dead who die in the Lord, even so saith the spirit; for they rest from their labors and their works do follow them."

HYMNS.

Rest for the toiling hand,
Rest for the anxious brow,
Rest for the weary, way-sore feet,
Rest from all labor now.

It is not death to bear
The stroke that sets us free
From earthly chain, to breathe the air
Of boundless liberty.

It is not death to fling
Aside this mortal dust,
And rise on strong, exulting wing
To live among the just.

We will not weep, for God is standing by us,
And tears will blind us to the blessed sight;
We will not doubt; if darkness still doth try us,
Our souls have promise of serenest light.

We will not faint; if heavy burdens bind us
They press no harder than our souls can bear:

The thorniest way is lying still behind us ;
　　We shall be braver for the past despair.

Oh, not in doubt shall be our journey's ending,
　　Sin, with its fears, shall leave us at the last ;
All its best hopes in glad fulfillment blending,.
　　Life shall be with us when the Death is past.

Help us, O Father, when the world is pressing
　　On our frail hearts that faint without their friend !
Help us, O Father ! let thy constant blessing
　　Strengthen our weakness till the joyful end.

ADDRESS.

Here we have met to perform this last sad act of love ; here in the fragrant breath of spring, amid freshening green, the opening of flowers, and the song of birds, on this pleasant slope opening to the sun, in this sacred earth in which his fathers sleep ; from this outlook so full of that beauty of scene, upon which his eyes so many times lingered, and where they dwelt with such fondness and delight, — here we have come with tearful hearts and loving hands to commit the dear form of our relative and friend to its final rest.

After a full life, long, and yet so short, filled with activity in the noblest of pursuits, the educating and up- lifting of mankind, world-wide reaching in its influence, crowned with success and honor, he has come to lie down in his final sleep upon this spot of earth, where his eyes first opened upon the strangeness of the world, and where again he was born into lofty aspirations and ambitions.

Rest and sleep, — sleep and rest ; these are the touching symbols ; these, the sweetest of words known to toiling and suffering humankind, are what we use to describe this last stage in our mortal journey, — this which is not death, but transition.

If a man die shall he live again ? Revelation answers, " Christ the divine has arisen." Eighteen Christian centuries have answered, and the great and good of all ages have answered. The human heart and human reason answer. Science answers that no particle of the universe can be destroyed. Can, then, the spirit which makes the human soul ?

· How great, then, is life ! change, transition, death, but through all, and in all, an ever-continuing life. In our memory and affections how strong and real is the life of our friend to-day ! How vivid he is in influence and power, — in that wide world wherein he moved and wrought. Can the influence of his good words and works ever have an end ? Not until you shall turn back time, and blot out the span of his mortal existence.

And I see him now, as I saw him so lately, in yonder cemetery, planning and working to beautify and protect it ; as I saw him here, at his house, filled with a certain homeish gladness to be among these scenes, with old neighbors and townsmen, — simple, honest, working people that he loved. I see him with his noble, illumined face, his frank and winning manner, his hearty clasp of the hand, his serious words lighted up with flashes of pleasantry, — the warm welcome of his whole soul ! I see in all his generous and sympathetic spirit, thoughtful of all but himself, constantly planning some individual or

public benefit, like the free public library which he established here in his native town.   And in these last years
I have seen him clothed in that gentle mist of divine
patience, visible, through his natural buoyancy of spirits,
only to loving eyes, with which he met his increasing
loss of sight.

So will that life he lived always exist in one form or
another upon the earth.   Thus living here, how much
more shall there always be life for him in some happy
sphere above and beyond.   It is these great and good
souls that quiet our doubting minds, that prove to us this
truth of immortal life.   To be forever with him we need
only to be like him.   Always, now and forever, we are
with, one with, in heart, mind, and soul, those whom we
are alike; no height, nor depth, nor distance, nor time,
can ever separate such as these.

Now, as companions and travelers, we part for a little
with our friend, who has finished one stage of the journey and taken on another.   Sweet, generous, gentle
spirit, hail, but not farewell! rather let us whisper our
loving "good-night" till we all meet at the dawn of the
great morning.

> I wage not any feud with Death,
>   For changes wrought on form and face;
>   No lower life that earth's embrace
> May breed with him can fright my faith.
>
> Eternal process moving on,
>   From state to state the spirit walks;
>   And these are but the shatter'd stalks,
> Or ruin'd chrysalis of one.

EULOGISTIC LETTERS.

EULOGISTIC LETTERS.

About two weeks after Dr. Philbrick's funeral, the *New England Journal of Education* published a memorial number, consisting of eulogistic letters from all parts of the country. These letters, perhaps, indicate as clearly as anything can the estimate in which Dr. Philbrick was held by the educators of America, and the warm place he filled in their hearts. Below are given many of these letters. Explanatory of the purpose of publishing these letters, there appeared in the memorial number of the *Journal*, under date of Feb. 18, 1886, the following

EDITORIAL.

It was our purpose to give a liberal share of the JOUR-NAL this week to tributes to the memory of Mr. Phil-brick ; but, so generous and prompt have been the responses, and so valuable are the reminiscences, reviews, and estimates of his life, that we most cheerfully sur-render our editorial, as well as other pages, to the words of high esteem and noble affection which flow from so many pens. It is most worthy of record that these contribu-tions are not fulsome eulogies, nor unbecoming praises of Mr. Philbrick. All bear, in their deepest meaning, honest and heartfelt testimonies to some trait, quality, or service, which are established by the mouths of many

ready witnesses. We had intended to add our own
humbler word to these, but must withhold it for another
opportunity, preferring that the brethren, who speak so
truly and eloquently, should express their sentiments of
appreciative affection.   Their contributions to his worth
form a monument as enduring as can be built, having for
its foundation, a noble, devoted, generous, Christian manhood. We shall be greatly surprised, if our readers in
all parts of our country do not welcome these tokens of
regard, which are not only personal to Mr. Philbrick as a
man and an educator, but are of greater moment to the
whole body of teachers, as the recognition of a professional spirit and devotion, which are the best evidence
that his life had a purpose, and that it was crowned with
most grátifying success. With Mann and Agassiz and
Page and Philbrick among our worthies, we certainly
have some reason to be proud of our calling, and of all
who bear the name of Teacher.

LETTER OF E. E. WHITE, LL.D.

The death of the noble Philbrick has touched me more
deeply than that of any other New England educator
since the death of Horace Mann, and Mr. Mann, as you
know, spent his last years in Ohio as president of An-
tioch College, thus adding to my high esteem for him the
felicity of a personal acquaintance.

I first met Dr. Philbrick in the superintendent's office
in Boston, the city so long and so highly honored by his
professional labors, and the acquaintance there formed
grew with passing years into an intimate friendship;

and, though the distance between our homes denied me the close personal fellowship enjoyed by his New England associates, I am sure that few of them think of his death with a deeper sense of personal bereavement. I have not only admired Dr. Philbrick for many years, but I have increasingly esteemed his wisdom, and leaned upon him for counsel and guidance. Few American educators have spoken or written fewer unripe views on education than he. He was blessed with that poise and catholicity of mind that enabled him to look on all sides of a complex truth, and especially a truth to be embodied in methods of teaching. If he were less enthusiastic than some others, it was because he saw more clearly their limitations. His apparent conservatism was the poise of deep insight and wide knowledge. He held firmly to the good that had been tested, while he sought for and welcomed better things.

His reports as superintendent of the Boston schools, so admirable in contents, spirit, and diction, and his more recent papers on current school questions, will be consulted a few years hence as the wisest contributions of these days. His comprehensive papers on " City School Systems," published in 1885 by the Bureau of Education, and on " School Reports," submitted to the Council last summer, embody wise experience, patient research, and profound wisdom. But I must leave a fitting recognition of Dr. Philbrick's great services in the cause of education to others. My heart calls me back to a simpler tribute of obligation and love.

When I assumed the principalship of a Cleveland

school many years ago, I was so fortunate as to take a "peep" into a Boston school, through the keen eyes of the lamented Cyrus Knowlton of Cincinnati. The school thus seen became an inspiring ideal, and greatly contributed to my success as a teacher. Years afterward I learned it was Mr. Philbrick's school that had been so vividly pictured to me, and so for a third of a century I have been his debtor. There now lies before me a precious letter from his stricken home, informing me that Dr. Philbrick wrote his name the last time to attest his friendship for me, and that my name was among the last words which he uttered. Thus the debt of long ago and this last touching honor span all the years between with inspiration and benediction!

A prince among American educators has fallen! Peace to his ashes, and consolation and blessings to the afflicted widow!

LETTER OF WM. T. HARRIS, LL. D.

I feel keenly the grief that comes to teachers and friends of education, at the announcement of Dr. Philbrick's death. There is an inner circle of personal friends who knew him and loved him and honored him, for both personal and professional reasons. There is an outer circle who knew him and respected him as a veteran authority in matters pertaining to education, and this circle includes the entire profession devoted to teaching and the management of schools, in every civilized country in the world. I would fain lay claim to belong to the inner circle, although I have never been officially connected with him. I knew him many years as a laborer in the same field of work. Indeed, my first acquaintance with him dated back to 1852, when I met him at an educational institute. I watched with eager interest his career as superintendent of the State system of Connecticut and subsequently of the schools of Boston.

His annual reports were luminous with insight into the relations of practical methods to the history of pedagogy. He was a city set upon a hill. He never wrote a paragraph without considering the relation of its doctrine to the theory and practice of the world. The effect of his writings, therefore, was a broadening one. Teachers learned from him to look at their work from an elevation, and to take in its perspective.

I have often noted his generosity toward his contemporaries. He seemed to take especial pleasure in crediting others with any good points that he could detect in their methods or theories. In this respect his influence was specially inspiring to young men ambitious to excel in their profession. I should lay great emphasis on this grand feature of his character as it appeared from a distance. I have no doubt that the memories of those who worked near him can supply innumerable examples of the manifestation of this noble trait.

There comes into my mind, as eminently fitting on the occasion of the death of a great teacher, the words from the prophet Daniel, quoted in the epitaph of Fichte on his tomb in Berlin : "The teachers shall shine as the brightness of the firmament, and they that turn many to righteousness as the stars for ever and ever."

LETTER OF JOHN G. WHITTIER.

I am glad to hear that the *Journal of Education* will issue a memorial number devoted to my honored friend, Dr. Philbrick, of this town. I had known of his educational work for many years, but had never the pleasure of his personal acquaintance until he took up his residence in my neighborhood. I found him a busy student, deeply interested in the cause to which his life had been devoted, but at the same time a genial, unpretending gentleman, and a very pleasant addition to our social circle.

The last time I saw him, some two months ago, he was suffering from partial blindness, but seemed in his usual good spirits. He was specially interested in the educational progress of Europe, and in the female colleges established recently in France. He warmly commended Wellesley College and its young and able president, and expressed great satisfaction at the auspicious opening of the Bryn Mawr College, in Philadelphia. He was deeply impressed with the imperative necessity of the education of all the people of the United States, irrespective of color or nationality, as the only sure safeguard of liberty and progress, regarding the ballot in the hands of ignorance a cause for serious apprehension of national dangers. A good and true man, who served his generation faithfully and successfully, he deserves to be held in grateful remembrance.

LETTER OF GEN. JOHN EATON, LL.D.

Your plan is most fit. But it would be easier to write a volume than "a word" exactly descriptive of Dr. Philbrick, or of my memories of him.

I first heard of him when I was fitting for college under Dr. Orcutt, his classmate. In my earliest knowledge of educators I read of Mr. Philbrick as a "Boston teacher," then as in Connecticut; and soon, again, as in Boston, and at the head of the city schools.

In returning East from my year's work in Ohio, I was accustomed to see for myself all I could of schools and leading teachers and educators. On my first return through Boston I learned much, through Nathan Bishop, of his first experience as superintendent in Providence and Boston. On my next visit I met Mr. Philbrick, and his strong characteristics impressed me deeply. In my mind were definite questions, some theoretical, others practical. In his answers there was no assumption of superiority, no brag, no *ex cathedra* announcements. He was a master, — strong, on the alert, but judicial, and employing the scientific methods for working out the great problems before him. He quoted what had been tried here and there, and failed or succeeded, and stated what he was trying, giving me most valuable facts and suggestions specially available for my study and practice. His mind had before it most abundant information and theories, but I specially felt his power to hold all in abeyance until their adoption in administration was clearly expedient.

I have been a debtor to Dr. Philbrick in education from the first. How many teachers obtained their first hints from him! From this experience of mine I readily saw later, when I referred foreign educators to him, how they were sure to report the great benefit they gained from a visit to him,

He did not put affairs out of joint. He administered city schools, but he studied profoundly the general principles of education, and saw how part fitted part and threw light upon the whole. Again and again I met foreign educators, after Dr. Philbrick's visit to Vienna, who could hardly find language strong enough to express their high opinion of him. Among them a most eminent inspector of normal schools in Belgium, who had taken the great step to call to his aid a lady as an assistant inspector, declared himself fully confirmed in his view by Dr. Philbrick's approval, and that he prized what he learned from Dr. Philbrick about education more than all else that he gained at Vienna.

Dr. Philbrick's representation of education at Paris, in 1878, was of the greatest possible service. He could do justice to any part of it. He won for us the confidence and respect of all inquirers, however humble or renowned. He and his exhibit, though small, were sought by the most eminent students of education. His great ability and attainments, his industry and devotion, his skill and aptness to teach, all served him well, and none who came went away unenlightened. He became a favorite American guest at distinguished gatherings. The honors conferred by the French and the "Doctor of Laws," by the Scotch University, and the remembrances which flowed in till the day of his death, were most deserved.

The French Commissioner to the New Orleans Exhibition made a special pilgrimage to Asylum Station, and could not restrain his lamentations when he learned that the Doctor was in New Hampshire, whither he could not go before the sailing of the vessel on which he had engaged passage.

The great benefits derived from him and his work by the Japanese are well known, and have been often acknowledged. Bishop Frazer, until his death, was the Doctor's admiring correspondent. Dr. Philbrick's marvelous power of seeing a situation in education, and meeting it, enabled him to give most timely counsel to those dealing with difficulties, old or new. How many state and city systems has he helped! He was quick to discover and recognize good work wherever done.

He set a high value upon associations for the promotion of education, as will be recognized by his frequent sacrifices to attend meetings and take part in them. His inspiring a great body of Eastern teachers to attend the National Association at Chicago will not be forgotten, and illustrates his ideas and activity. What an impulse they left behind them, and how much they learned and enjoyed!

He specially aided in educational journalism as editor, writer, and adviser. Who that saw him at Saratoga, nearly blind, and led about by his devoted wife, can forget him, or his masterly paper, or his wise and delightful conversation! Even after his retirement to his country home, no great movement in education escaped him, whether affecting the entire country, or a state, or city, or institution, and he had the courage of his convictions; he stood by his colors. His works will remain to honor him and instruct coming generations. What a set of city reports is that which he made of the Boston schools!

Every one is a study. When has there appeared so
much wisdom in a single pedagogical paper as in the circular prepared by him for the Bureau of Education, and
published by it!

His life covered a most marked period in the progress
of education, in which he was a most effective actor, and
in which his name will ever be associated. He gathered
the richest fruit for his chosen profession to the last.
Teachers everywhere may well honor him and emulate
his virtues.

LETTER OF JOHN S. CLARK.

I had the pleasure of knowing Dr. Philbrick very well
for the last twenty years of his life, and of one feature of
his work I may, perhaps, be permitted to speak with
exceptional knowledge. Among the prominent educators of the country he was the first to perceive the value
of art education in general education, as well as the first
to take active steps toward its promotion. I think it is
generally conceded that the movement for the study of
drawing in public schools, which, within the last fifteen
years, has extended over the whole country, had its beginning in Boston in 1870. How important a movement
this has been, and what a development it has given to
education in many directions, is well known to all observ-
ers of public schools for the last ten years. I do not
think I do injustice to the many gentlemen who took a
deep interest in starting the movement in Massachusetts,
when I say that the leading spirit in the movement was
Dr. Philbrick. He was at that time superintendent of

the public schools of Boston, and a member of the State Board of Education. My intimate acquaintance with him began about this time, and, above all others, he seemed to have clear ideas in regard to how the work should be begun in the schools, and how it should be developed. In my various consultations with him he surprised me, not only by the thoroughness of his observation in regard to what had been done abroad, but also by his clear comprehension of what was necessary to be done here before any success could be expected.

While his official reports at this time bear evidence of his earnest conviction in regard to the importance of drawing and art education generally, they give little indication of the very earnest personal efforts he was making in every direction to promote the undertaking, both in the city and in the state. ' To Dr. Philbrick more than to any other one person are we indebted for our Massachusetts Normal Art School. The necessity for such an institution became apparent to him at the outset of the movement, and his experience as an educator enabled him to see, with perhaps greater clearness than others, its necessity in order to carry on the work throughout the state. It was through his instrumentality, mainly, that Mr. Walter Smith was induced to come to Boston in 1872, and in the early years of Mr. Smith's labors he had Dr. Philbrick's earnest support.

The art movement in education, which he did so much to inaugurate, engaged his deepest attention to the last. The closing years of his official life in Boston showed increased interest in the subject ; and since his retirement at Danvers he has evinced the liveliest interest in the spread of drawing throughout the country, and I have been in the habit of consulting him frequently in regard to various educational points that have arisen in my own work. I always found him full to repletion of wise counsel; and I never left him without feeling myself his debtor to an extent that could not be paid. His presence at the National Association at Saratoga was especially memorable by reason of his visit to the Art Exhibition. In the excellent work there exhibited from the schools of Worcester, St. Louis, Chicago, and Quincy, he took the greatest delight. He was able to see the development that had taken place within the last few years in the study of form and drawing, and, as he expressed himself, " It was the realization of what he could only hope for fifteen years ago." As I knew the deep interest he took in this particular line of educational work, I was greatly pleased that his partially dimmed eyes were gladdened by a sight so full of promise to the future of public education before they were closed forever.

There are so many who will pay fitting tribute to Dr. Philbrick's eminent public services that I have felt like speaking only on that feature in his work with which I was intimately acquainted. He was a leader and a pioneer in the art movement in education which is now going so successfully over the country; and in all stages of its progress his labor and his counsel have been invaluable.

Fully cognizant of his efforts in behalf of this feature in education, and his faith in its future development, it gives me great pleasure to add this tribute to his memory.

LETTER OF GILMAN H. TUCKER.

On New Year's Day, 1853, I went as a boy from my country home in New Hampshire to New Britain, Conn., to be under the immediate instruction and direction of Mr. John D. Philbrick, who, as assistant superintendent of common schools for the state of Connecticut, had assumed the charge of the State Normal and Training Schools located in that place. My uncle, who responded to my desire to "go away to school" by sending me there, had a very high estimate of the value of the teaching and influence of Mr. Philbrick, and, I remember, quoted some *Plutarch* saying, that it was regarded as the greatest good fortune that a youth was born at a time when he could have the teaching of Socrates. He rightly judged that nothing was so important to one in obtaining an education as to come under the influence of a gifted teacher and a great and good man.

From this time commenced a personal intimacy which, growing into a close friendship, lasted to the end of Mr. Philbrick's life. Later, after completing school and college, as a young man "beginning the world," I was for several years a member of his household in Boston, and since have always been a frequent and welcome visitor in his home. In these thirty-three years what have I not owed to him as teacher and friend!

As a teacher Mr. Philbrick placed before himself the highest ideal. No man could ever be more in love with, or more completely devoted to, his profession. He read and studied its greatest authors, and associated with its best exponents. And his mind was so receptive and so practical that he assimilated all, so that the fruit of his knowledge always appeared in his daily work. His plans were always broad, and his system founded on sound principles. Teaching was to him a great thing, — a philosophy; not a mere theory or art, but both and more, — the love and pursuit of wisdom. Its aim was to develop intelligent, well rounded out, and evenly balanced men and women.

The governing principle of his own life was not merely seeking increase of knowledge, — though none pursued that with more industry and success, — but *growth in wisdom*. His whole career exemplified this, and he became the Franklin among educators. He was, in his ripe years, certainly the wisest man in his profession of public educator in this whole country, if not in the world.

As a teacher he was a very strong personality. His presence was always a sunshine and stimulus, his enthusiasm generous and unbounded, and dull indeed must be the mind not waked into activity and ambition by contact with his own. He had a real, personal interest in the individual students, studied and recognized their peculiarities, and instructed and influenced them accordingly. The breadth, and I may say *height*, of his teaching was a peculiarity. He was constantly broadening and elevating the minds of his pupils, and, without noise or demonstration, continually building up character. The purest and noblest aims were *caught*, not taught, by magnetic contact with his own clear and lofty character. The true teacher is so much greater than a book as a living organism is greater than a lifeless machine. Fortunate those who were pupils of this great teacher, and greater man, and more fortunate to have carried his impress with them through life.

To speak of Dr. Philbrick as a friend, — and here, with me, only affection can speak. He was a very social person by nature, and a wide acquaintance among the best had afforded him means to highly cultivate himself in this direction. He was a superior conversationalist, and his flow of talk was always rich and entertaining. Pleasant, genial, and kind-hearted to all, to his intimates he was warm, sympathetic, generous, self-forgetting, and devoted. He idealized his friends. He did not see their faults, or, if he did, they were overlooked. He dwelt upon their abilities and virtues. How he loved to recount their good qualities, and what great things they could accomplish if they dared and tried! How often his cheerful courage and generous confidence carried hope and faith to his friends, which enabled them to accomplish work which had otherwise been unaccomplished! His sympathetic helpfulness, extended during his whole life toward young men and women who sought his aid and advice, especially those beginning the profession of teaching, must be remembered by thousands in all parts of the country who were benefited by it. His confidence once given was perfect unless basely betrayed, and no man was a better judge of character or less often mistaken. While he understood the maxim that to have a friend one must be one, he constantly helped his friends in all possible ways when he knew there could be no return in kind. He gave more than he took, — he had so much to give, — and it seemed to enrich the giver as well as the receiver.

In his home he was brightness itself, thoughtful always of others, and here his life was as tender and beautiful as his public life was great and strong. As a host, joining with his worthy wife, — always so true a helpmeet to him in contributing to a perfect home, — what pleasure or comfort for a guest was ever overlooked, or what warmth of welcome wanting !

Such, but so imperfectly sketched, is a glimpse of the great and good man, John Dudley Philbrick. His earthly life is ended. May Heaven enrich the world with another like him !

LETTER OF THOMAS H. BARNES.

There are some people who must be known intimately to be understood and appreciated. Mr. Philbrick was one of these. Those who saw him merely upon the platform or at a distance were inclined to think he was overestimated by his friends ; but those who came into intimate relations with him very soon learned that they were enjoying the acquaintance of a man of no ordinary mind, and one who formed his opinions with due deliberation and undoubted evidence and authority. I never really knew him until I was brought into the close relation which exists between a master and the superintendent ; then I learned how much of a man I was dealing with, and how sound he was upon all matters relating to education.

When one knowing Mr. Philbrick well differed from him upon educational subjects, it became him to well weigh his own views before deciding that Mr. Philbrick was in error; for he would always be aware that Mr. Philbrick never came to his conclusions hastily, but always had well-grounded reasons for the opinions he entertained. He was a man who could be approached by the humblest of educators and be kindly received, for he was a large-hearted man, and had a pleasant and encouraging word for all who desired advice and were trying to help themselves.

Although I knew him well, yet I was surprised to find that he was even better known out of New England than in it. When I was in Washington, in the winter of 1877 –78, just as he was completing his preparations to go to France as representative of the educational interests of this country, I gave myself the pleasure of calling on him at his headquarters at the rooms of the National Bureau of Education. I met there General Eaton and other well-known educators, and I found that he was accorded by them the highest place as a man of sound, practical views upon education. It was a matter of great surprise to them that Boston would consent to accept his resignation as superintendent of our schools, but they felt that Boston's loss would be the nation's gain.

Mr. Philbrick as a writer upon education had no superior, as is clearly indicated by his many and voluminous reports, which show a thorough acquaintance with the progress of education in this and other countries, and are in themselves a complete history of the same.

I really wish I could say something worthy the name and fame of Dr. Philbrick, but, as others will write of his merits as a man and an educator, I will mention only one or two items among the many reminiscences I have of him.

After he had been appointed master of the Quincy School he visited the college from which he graduated, and some of the students were introduced to him. Such was his zeal and enthusiasm in the profession to which he was to devote his life that many of us were induced to choose teaching as a vocation. I thought if I could only be one of his corps of teachers, have him for a guide, I should be content to labor a lifetime under such a director.

When teaching in a distant state, I heard that there was a vacancy in the Quincy School; I immediately came to see Mr. Philbrick, but found I was too late, for another had obtained the place. But my journey to Boston was not for naught, as I saw Mr. Philbrick in school, and noticed what a power he had over his teachers and boys, — what an interest he awakened in his intercourse with others, and how splendidly he "kept school." I returned to my country school a better teacher, determined, if possible, to teach in Boston, and learn how to teach by knowing and watching Mr. Philbrick. I was connected with the Boston schools when he was master, and I lost no opportunity to visit his school and learn of him. I never went to his school without feeling my own deficiency and the infinite resources at his command to make an excellent school.

He was willing and anxious to help young teachers, and we looked up to him as a safe adviser, a wise counsellor, and a true friend.

During his first term of service as superintendent I was one of the Boston masters, and I know how we looked to him for direction and advice, — never in vain. He took a deep interest in us and in our individual schools, and often commended us if we tried to develop a subject in which, at the time, he was specially interested. He had no hobbies to ride, but believed that education meant a development of the whole man, mentally, physically, and morally. He endeavored to stimulate one's noblest faculties to action, to incite him to form good habits, and to mould an excellent character, — to make him what he should be, a whole man ; but sometimes he laid particular stress on a certain subject when he thought it had been neglected.

He always was popular with the Boston masters because he confided in us, trusted us, and thought we knew how to manage our individual schools. He let us do as we pleased if we pleased to do right, but he was not slow to point out our faults, and kindly helped us to correct them.

He did a noble work for our schools, and not alone for our schools, but for the cause of good learning. He was the teachers' friend, and did much to make the profession of teaching noble and honorable. His reputation as a true educator will increase wherever true culture is known and appreciated.

The name of Dr. Philbrick is a benediction to us who still labor and wait.

To the workers in the broad West the death of Dr. Philbrick came as a bereavement. For many years we have looked on and criticised his work, but with an ever-increasing conviction that his plans were well laid and his methods comprehensive. No one knows better than those who have labored in fields similar to the one he so faithfully cultivated, how hard the task of organizing and administering city schools,—hard indeed, when old and deep-rooted prejudices must be overcome. Some of us at the West have felt the wisdom of his counsels, without realizing the benefit to us of being able to plant the good seed in virgin soil. We may, on this account, have been ready to attribute to him tardiness of movement. Looking back over the past, we see no retrogression, but steady progress. What fitter tribute can we pay to the memory of our departed brother than this? In labors abundant, not always appreciated as they deserved, Dr. Philbrick moved on serenely, conscious that he was right, and in this was his success.

LETTER OF ROBERT C. METCALF.

My earliest recollections of Boston schools are connected with the administration of Mr. Philbrick as superintendent. The number of schools in the city thirty years ago was so small when compared with the number at the present time that a visit from the superintendent was by no means so rare an occurrence as now. I remember well those visits, and the words of encouragement that were to me so helpful. Many a time has the recollection of them prompted me to encourage others by seeing only what was worthy of commendation. Most of us know of vastly more faults than we are able to correct; and there is little need that they should be pointed out by superiors.

Mr. Philbrick was kind-hearted and sympathetic. An excellent teacher himself, he recognized and appreciated the good work of teachers under his supervision. A man of broad views, he labored steadily to systematize the work of the Boston schools. A close student in educational matters, he was thoroughly acquainted with the school systems of other cities and of other countries. He believed that good schools implied good teachers and wise supervision. To procure the former he was instrumental in establishing the city normal school, and he hoped to secure the latter by bringing the primary and grammar departments under one head, and placing one principal over both.

Under the superintendency of Mr. Philbrick the most cordial relations were established between the different schools of the city. The masters were no longer rivals,— they were brethren, and have remained such to this day.

The schoolmasters of Boston owe a debt of gratitude to Mr. Philbrick that even the love which they lavished upon him when alive, the heart-felt grief which followed him to the grave, and the tender recollections which cluster about his memory, can never repay.

It was my privilege to know Mr. Philbrick as a friend, a neighbor, a townsman, and an educator. From a child his name was familiar to me, but I did not know him personally till 1862, when I came to Boston for an extended visit. His large-heartedness and his great wisdom in all educational matters at once impressed me, and I was very soon led by his influence into the public schools of Boston. From that time till his death he has ever been ready with his counsel and encouragement, and as a teacher I owe him more than any other person excepting the late Lewis B. Monroe.

I will not here dwell, however, upon the many pleasant memories connected with his professional work, but will allude briefly to a phase of his life not so well known to most of his educational friends, — his loyalty to his native town, and his attachment to the old homestead. Amid all his successes he never lost his love for his boy-hood home, nor his interest in the humblest of his neighbors, and his devotion as a son and a brother was beautiful in the extreme, commanding the admiration of all who knew him in this relation. He used to say, in speaking of the Deerfield home, " It is the prettiest spot in the world to me ; you ought to go out in the field just beyond the house and *see* what a view there is ! "

Through his influence each school district in the town was long ago supplied with an *Unabridged Dictionary*, and improved seats and desks were put into the high school. He saw the need of a public library, and in-

duced a wealthy gentleman of New York, a former resi-
dent of the town, to give the money, himself selecting all
the books. It is called the Philbrick-James Library. In
his own school district he has annually appropriated a
sum for a Fourth-of-July picnic, and has, when possible,
been present himself.

We had thought to enjoy his wise counsel many years,
and to do much to express our gratitude for his benefac-
tions. He is to be laid at rest with his father and
mother in the family burial ground. on the old place,
which he had just surrounded with a unique granite wall,
in English style. Here we shall gladly, every summer,
place upon his grave the old-fashioned flowers he so
much loved.

LETTER OF JUSTIN H. SMITH.

Early in 1878 Mr. Philbrick was selected by the government to direct the National Exhibit of Education at
the Universal Exposition, opening in Paris on April 1st
of that year. The authorities were scantily informed of
the need for such an exhibit, and of the magnitude of the
undertaking; the decision was late, the appropriation
meager, the educational public indifferent or disheart-
ened. Had there not been in Mr. Philbrick full knowledge, prompt action, ample resources, and resolute
enthusiasm, the enterprise must have proved a failure.
Warmly and ably supported by General Eaton, the Commissioner of Education, he was able to sail the 20th of
March with an abundance of choice material secured.

Arrived at Paris, full of enthusiasm, he found he had

not a foot of space, and was only one of half a hundred eager and disappointed applicants. The difficulty was met with characteristic patience, tact, and perseverance, and at last he was given a space of about 21 by 25 feet, in which to unfold his representative exhibit of the foremost educational country of the world.

In organizing and in conducting the department he was indefatigable and sagacious, always enthusiastic, cheerful, and philosophic, never losing sight of his constituents' interests, while continually in demand to confer with his colleagues of the Jury, attend social and official gatherings, deliver addresses at the Sorbonne and elsewhere, explain the exhibit to deputations of teachers, and meet his professional friends from Great Britain, France, Germany, Austria, Spain, Italy, Sweden, Russia, Japan, Canada, and Australia. At the close of the Exposition his collection was solicited by the French government, and, substantially a unit, was permanently established in the palace that contains Venus de Milo and masterpieces of Raphael, Murillo, Titian, and Rubens.

Mr. Philbrick brought back to America for his constituents 121 high awards, — more than any other country except France herself received, — and for himself the cross of the Legion of Honor, the gold palm of the *Université de France*, the Doctorate of Laws from the ancient University of St. Andrews, and, — the only reward he sought, — the respect and esteem of the most eminent educators in all the civilized countries of the globe.

To this work, as to all his professional duties, Mr. Philbrick was ardently devoted, and he gave it the most a man could give, — himself, — for to its success he consciously sacrificed the continuance of his public career, and many of the hopes he had cherished for his declining years.

LETTER OF HON. JOHN W. DICKINSON.

Mr. John D. Philbrick was born in Deerfield, N. H., on the 27th of May, 1818, and died at Danvers, Mass., on the 2d of February, 1886. Mr. Philbrick received his collegiate education at Dartmouth College, from which institution he graduated in 1842. While a student in college, he was noted for his industry and his perseverance. He entered college for a purpose, and he never lost sight of it until it was fully accomplished. During his sophomore year he chose teaching for his life-work, and from that time he studied with reference to preparing himself for the duties of his chosen profession.

On graduating from college he came to Boston and entered at once upon his chosen work, beginning as assistant teacher in the Latin school in Roxbury. The same qualities of mind and heart exhibited themselves in his practical life as a teacher, that had distinguished him through the years of his college course as learner. He was industrious in preparing his daily tasks and persevering in the application of his methods of teaching and control.

His success as a teacher attracted attention, and in 1844 he was transferred from the Roxbury school to the English High School. In 1845 he was made master of the Mayhew School. Three years later he was appointed

to organize the Quincy School, the first of the present
system of grammar schools of the city.   In 1852 he was
called from Boston to New Britain, Conn., to organize
the State Normal School, established two years before in
that town, for the training of teachers of the public
schools.   By an act of the Connecticut legislature, passed
in 1849, the office of Superintendent of Common Schools
and that of principal of the State Normal School were
united.   Mr. Philbrick accepted the twofold office, and
did all in his power to perform well the responsible duties
committed to his care.   As principal of an important educational institution, and as superintendent of a system
of schools, he did enough for Connecticut to eventually
provide for her public schools better trained teachers, and
for the teachers themselves a more generous support.

By invitation of the school committee of Boston, he
came back to Massachusetts in 1857, and commenced
what proved to be the great work of his life, — the re-
organization and direction of the public schools of the
city.   Mr Philbrick was superintendent of the public
schools of Boston from 1857 to 1874, and again from 1876
to 1878, and when he resigned his office he left these
schools the best organized and conducted public educational institutions in this or any other country.

Mr. Philbrick performed some important educational
service outside of his labors as superintendent of schools.
He was for ten years a member of the State Board of
Education, during which time he gave full sympathy and
cordial support to the State Normal Schools, then in the
infancy of their existence.   He was appointed by the

government to represent our educational affairs at the Vienna Exhibition, in 1873, and again at the great Paris Exhibition in 1878, of which he made elaborate and able reports. He organized and superintended our own educational exhibit at Philadelphia, in 1876, and did his work with so much skill and good judgment, that the products of the Massachusetts public schools were judged to be of the highest excellence.

Mr. Philbrick has contributed much to our educational literature by his able public addresses, and by his valuable school reports, which have embodied his best thoughts on a great variety of educational topics. These reports will be read, I am sure, with increasing interest by all educators who have access to them, as the years go by.

And, finally, I find that Mr. Philbrick was a member of that association of gentlemen, who, interested in the professional applications of science, and in the practical and fine arts, began to form those ideas, which, after struggling for a long time for an opportunity to make a material expression of themselves, finally, on the eighth day of April, 1862, were organized into the Massachusetts Institute of Technology, — an institution that introduced at once a new and most important element into our systems of education. From the day of the organization of this distinguished institution to the time of his death, I believe Mr. Philbrick was a member of its corporation and of its committee on instruction. He was an earnest and intelligent friend of the Institute, for he was deeply interested in its objects and its methods.

In his written words, found at the close of what he thought to be his last report to the School Committee of Boston, are expressed the great principles of action by which he was moved throughout his educational life : —

" For upward of thirty years, — all but four in this city, — I have occupied, without the intermission of a day, various positions of service in connection with the public schools. Here my professional career has been run. It was the career of my choice, and my highest ambition. My heart has been in it. It has afforded me the desired opportunity for making my humble contribution to the general welfare. I am thankful for it. I shall never cease to be grateful to all who have co-operated with me in my efforts to make the Boston public schools the best in the world ; and I will venture to say that I ask no ill thing for the cause, when on parting from such place, I pray that whomsoever you shall choose to succeed me, he may resemble me in the uprightness of his intentions, and surpass me in the degree of his abilities."

LETTER OF HON. MELLEN CHAMBERLAIN.

I have a vague recollection of the late John D. Philbrick when he was preparing for college at Pembroke Academy, but my intimacy with him began when I entered Dartmouth College, in 1840, where he preceded me by two years.

I succeeded him as teacher of a district school at Danvers, and soon found in my pupils indications that they had been under the instruction of a strong mind, but otherwise I had no particular knowledge of his distinctive life-work. He was in one line of business and I in another, but I always watched his career and rejoiced in his success. I knew him best as a man, and I think I knew him well.

At one time he thought of entering the legal profession, and made some progress in his reading. Had he finally given himself to the law he would, I have no doubt, attained to great eminence in it. He always impressed me as a man of extraordinary grasp and vigor of understanding, equable in its manifestations, and depending but little upon external conditions. His results were reached less by intuition than by labor, but he had great power for labor, and honestly applied it to the work in hand. I should be much surprised to learn that he ever neglected a known duty, or was satisfied with merely its perfunctory performance. He seemed to keep before his eyes in all his work the highest attainment.

His moral qualities were no less marked. He had ambition for honorable distinction, but none other would have given him the slightest satisfaction, for his mind was thoroughly honest. He was a firm friend, — no one was more so, — and his judgments of others were generally correct; or, if there was any tendency to err, it was on the right side. He had the power of inspiring others to excel themselves, and, by so doing, he acquired many faithful coadjutors in his great work.

Of my own personal relations to Mr. Philbrick I do not trust myself to speak. When he died the cause of education lost one of its most able and devoted friends, and there are thousands who mourn his loss.

LETTER OF WM. A. MOWRY, Ph.D.

John D. Philbrick may well be called the apostle of public school education.   When he was a young man he devoted himself to the cause of education.   He determined to make it his life-work, and he adhered to that resolution to the end of an active and an honorable career.   For forty years he was closely identified with the interests of popular education ; and during most of that long period he held responsible positions in Boston.   As teacher in grammar, high, and normal schools he was ever studying and applying the highest principles of pedagogy and psychology.   As superintendent, whether of city or state schools, he was always foremost in the discussion of fundamental principles which should govern in reference to the organization, courses of study, methods of teaching, and all that pertained to the work of the schools.   Now that he has gone to rest, and the leading men who have been most intimately acquainted with his work reflect upon his chief qualities and characteristics, they will agree that above all men he was familiar with all that belonged to the province of educational affairs.

He was thoroughly acquainted with the schools of Boston.   He knew every detail of their organization, their condition, their history, and their prospects.   He was equally at home in regard to the schools of the world. The peculiarities of education in France, in Great Britain, in Germany, Austria, or St. Petersburg, were as clear to his mind as the alphabet or the multiplication table. He was no less familiar with the whole history and purpose of education in the past. Upon all these subjects his mind was a storehouse of wisdom, filled to overflowing, and the door standing wide open to all who desired to avail themselves of his accumulated knowledge. Probably there is no man in the world, now living, who possesses so full, so valuable, so minute, and so exact a knowledge of all educational history and principles, experiments and practices, as John D. Philbrick carried to the grave with him.

Another characteristic of Dr. Philbrick was his absolute devotion to truth. He was always and everywhere, and under all circumstances, true to his convictions. He was the soul of honor and uprightness. He was a true friend, never failing in time of need. This is a great thing to say of a man in this age of the world. The number of lamentable failures to come up to this standard in these times is so great that the life of a true man, a firm friend, always reliable and to be relied upon, is a marked life. All this was Mr. Philbrick. Now that he is silent in death, no man will dare to say, " He betrayed me," or " He failed me in the day of need." Beside he was especially the warm, personal friend to the young teacher. The time would fail to tell the instances that come to the mind where he has proved himself a true friend to some young man who needed a word of encouragement, appreciation, or caution. He was also always honorable as an opponent. Never would he take any undue advantage, or resort to any questionable methods to accomplish his ends. Bold, aggressive, manly, he was at the same time simple, ingenuous, honest, and straightforward.

His reputation was deservedly world-wide. His name was a household word among educational men, not only in New England, the South, the great Northwest, and on the Pacific slope, but also in England, France, Germany, Austria, Russia, China, and Japan. The present high reputation of the schools of Boston, the world over, depends, probably, more upon what John D. Philbrick has done for them and written and said about them than upon any other cause.

He had a remarkable judgment of men. Rarely did he err in his estimate of men or measures. He was always a wise counselor. Above all he was a devout man. With no cant, no show, no pretension, he was a sincere, humble, devout worshiper of God. The fundamental sentiment of his life is voiced in that beautiful hymn attributed to Addison, which he learned in his boyhood, which was ever sweet to his ear, and which was so impressively sung at the close of his funeral services : —

> " The spacious firmament on high,
> With all the blue ethereal sky,
> And spangled heavens, — a shining frame, —
> Their Great Original proclaim.

> *   *   *   *   *

> " In reason's ear they all rejoice,
> And utter forth a glorious voice ;
> Forever singing, as they shine, —
> ' The Hand that made us is divine.' "

As early as 1857 and 1858 the schoolhouse on Bedford street, Boston, became too narrow for the accommodation of the Latin and English High Schools, which were occupying it. The addition of another story was only a temporary relief. The schoolhouse on Mason street, abandoned by the Girls' High and Normal School, was brought into requisition ; then the Bowditch, on South street ; last of all, the Primary schoolhouse on Harrison avenue.

Dr. Philbrick declared the necessity of a new building for these two schools in his "Third Semi-annual Report," in 1861. As time advanced, and the necessity was beyond question, he became more urgent in his importunities for relief. He saw the need of a building for the future, and not simply for the present. At last the City Council, upon the recommendation of the School Board, voted to purchase a lot of land upon which to erect the largest schoolhouse in America, if not in the world.

The great fire of 1872 and the financial crisis of 1873 delayed operations till the election of Mr. F. O. Prince as mayor. In his first inaugural he proposed to plan for the erection of a building, without increasing the tax levy or the city debt.

Mr. George A. Clough, the city architect at that time, entered into the enterprise with the heartiest zeal, encouraged and aided by Dr. Philbrick, whose knowledge of schoolhouse architecture in Europe, — especially in

Vienna, — and of the needs of Boston, was most valuable in forming and completing the plan of the proposed building. Mr. Clough writes thus : —

" The earliest impressions that I received upon school architecture were from Dr. Philbrick, as far back as 1871, and now, after fifteen years' experience, I have had an opportunity to see that his views were far in advance of all other writers upon the subject in this country. In reviewing my experience, I find myself constantly associated with the early views of Dr. Philbrick."

The schoolhouse was erected within the limits of the appropriation, and is a very useful auxiliary to the school system of Boston. It is indeed a large structure, but thoroughly substantial, and excites the admiration of all visitors. Dr. Philbrick lived to see the building occupied by the two schools above named, and by various evening schools, and to have the satisfaction of knowing that it was not too large.

While we are indebted to many municipal officers and private citizens for their deep interest in this project, yet no one could more justly claim the credit of urging and aiding the prosecution of it, from the beginning to the very end, than the lamented Dr. Philbrick.

All interested in high school education, and especially the graduates and pupils of the Latin and English High Schools, will ever cherish his memory for what he did for the welfare of these two schools. But no one knew better than he that it was not an imposing structure that made the school. Others will speak of his great and continuous influence, through a long life, upon the cause of education in its more direct and positive forms, and show that this influence extended wherever popular education exists.

LETTER OF SAMUEL ELIOT, LL.D.

My acquaintance with Dr. Philbrick was but slight until we were connected, twenty years ago, in the American Social Science Association. In the rather nebulous mass of that body there was a very distinctly formed nucleus devoted to education, and this attracted him. He shared in the discussions of the Department Committee, attended the general meetings, spoke at them, and wrote for them. There were not many really active members. Such as took part, unpremeditatedly and often unhappily, in annual meetings, and then disappeared from the sight of their associates for a twelvemonth, were the rule. He was one of the exceptions, and showed his interest in the less public work of the association throughout the year. He was regarded as an educational authority, and his opinions, if not always followed, were always respected. He represented what is called the practical side. Other members took views that may have seemed larger, and were certainly more inspiring to some of us; but he stood intelligibly and strongly for progress that might be made at once, while that which they urged needed a long, in some instances a very long preparation. Perhaps this contrast would have faded had the educational life of the association continued, but it came to a pause, if not to an end, and those interested in it, Agassiz, Pierce, Philbrick, and the rest, were separated.

A year or two later I was unexpectedly called to the charge of one of the Boston schools, — I might say, one of Dr. Philbrick's schools, for it was one he had done much to strengthen, and it had recently removed to a new building which he had exerted himself to plan and to secure. This brought me face to face with him as superintendent, and I could see from within what I had hitherto seen from without. My observations increased my regard for him and for the work he had done. He held a position strong in sixteen years of solid service. His opinions, generally speaking, were dominant in the school committee, at that time a more numerous body than the present board. Many of the masters and teachers in the schools owed their places more or less to him. Many of the schoolhouses had been built under his direction. The courses of study in all grades had been laid out or modified by him more than by any other individual. The system of public instruction had just been completed to his satisfaction by the independent establishment of a normal school. It was a triumphant moment in his career, and there were few, perhaps none, to dispute the success of his administration. Closer scrutiny might show, or appear to show, deficiencies. Education had become somewhat mechanical. The schools, as a whole, were possibly too much like a vast machine. It was the penalty, one may say, of an organization that had been painfully perfected, and in consequence, it may be, of the struggles required to perfect it, had become too much of an end and too little of a means. But, whatever might be thought of the system, no one could question the zeal or the ability of its head. He was seen, or heard, or felt, in every part of it. Its interests were his, and he was quick to perceive where they were threatened, or how they could be advanced. He was contented with it, yet by no means so blindly as to be indifferent to its improvement. On the contrary he was unwearied in suggesting and in promoting such changes as he thought better than existing things. There is nothing in the present system, from the plan of a school building through all the offices of administration and instruction, and all classes of pupils, that does not feel, whether consciously or unconsciously, the touch of his hand, — a hand that has not vanished, and we may say will never vanish, from the Boston schools.

Of Dr. Philbrick's personal traits there are others to speak more fully. Let me but speak of one, and this is the generosity with which he welcomed a new associate in his labors. I could not forget if I would, — and assuredly I would not, — the cordial kindness he showed me when I became one of the schoolmasters under him. He made it easier for me to enter upon a field of work, not new in substance, but utterly new in form, and in which I might have found greater difficulties but for his support. He resigned his office for a time while I was at my post, and I wrote him a note of regret which was wholly genuine. The last time I met him for any conversation by ourselves, he said, " I have been reading the lines you sent me in 1874." " I am glad of it," I answered, "for I can say now I meant every word I wrote then."

I am glad to pay my humble tribute to the memory of our late distinguished fellow-citizen, John D. Philbrick, LL.D., in view of his high personal character, and of his valuable services in the cause of education.

When I became a member of the Board of Education, in 1869, he had already rendered some years of service in that body. His large experience in various positions in the educational field eminently qualified him to promote, by his counsels, the most important interests of the Commonwealth. As a teacher in the public schools in early life, and in the higher schools in later years ; as superintendent of the public schools of Boston, which were in no small measure transformed during his administration, and very largely through his influence ; and as Commissioner of the International Exhibition at Vienna, in 1873, affording him rare opportunities for becoming widely acquainted with institutions and methods of instruction both at home and abroad, — he became possessed of such treasures of knowledge as made his services in the Board of Education of especial value.

One of the most marked departures from the customary course of common school studies, during the term of Dr. Philbrick's membership of the board, was the introduction, into the schools, of elementary instruction in industrial drawing. In response to a petition from some of our foremost citizens, seconded by the Board of Education, the legislature, in 1870, passed an act introducing industrial drawing into the school curriculum in cities and towns containing more than ten thousand inhabitants. But brief experience under the law made it apparent that special preparation of teachers for this work was necessary to give definiteness of aim and adaptation of methods to the end in view.

Out of this discovery, among other instrumentalities, grew the State Normal Art School. In 1873 an appropriation of $9,000 was made for that purpose, and rooms, entirely inadequate, in the two upper stories, — one being the attic, — of 33 Pemberton Square, an ordinary dwelling-house, were assigned for the school. Out of this very humble beginning has grown an institution which is both an honor to Massachusetts and a blessing to the whole country. Appreciating this honor and usefulness, the State, in 1885, unconditionally set apart a piece of land at the corner of Newbury and Exeter streets, worth from $50,000 to $60,000, for the site of a suitable building for the school, and appropriated $85,000 for the erection of the building itself, which has already been put under contract.

The beginnings of this enterprise, now so full of usefulness and promise, were not secured without much thought, study, and argument, repeated year after year, by the Board of Education, in all the earlier of which labors Dr. Philbrick bore a conspicuous part. The school was opened in the autumn of 1873. During the first year of its history he held the responsible position of chairman of its board of visitors, and would doubtless have been continued in that office had not his membership of the Board of Education terminated. All who have been associated with Dr. Philbrick in these various labors, I feel warranted in saying, hold his memory in very high esteem.

I had the pleasure of Mr. Philbrick's acquaintance for nearly forty-eight years. We first met at Hanover, N. H., as students of Dartmouth College. Several things served to make our acquaintance speedy, and to intensify it from that day until the closing days of his life.

His father, the late Rev. Peter Philbrick, of Deerfield, N. H., and my father, as well as Mr. Philbrick and myself, were members of the same religious people, — a denomination about that time becoming interested in establishing several institutions of learning, such as academies or seminaries.

It is not for me to say anything about John D. Philbrick's great work in bringing up the public schools of Boston to their present high standard, — a standard that makes them, I am safe in saying, a model for the world to pattern after. Neither am I called upon to speak of his labors in foreign lands in behalf of the cause of education. Others among his many friends who know what he has done for this cause at home and abroad (for he yet speaketh) will do justice to him in this respect.

It is for me, in few words, to speak of his interest in the work of founding the school over which I have had the honor to preside from the beginning. It is over thirty-one years since the work of founding this college was begun, and, whatever part I have had in establishing

and managing it, I have always had Mr. Philbrick at my
right hand as a friend and adviser. He took pride in the
fact that the religious people with whom his honored
father was during his life connected, are laying the foun-
dations of a college yet to rank among the first in the
country. It should be said that this college had his
heart, his purse, and his vote. He was a trustee for ten
years, from 1873 to 1883.

All who knew Mr. Philbrick know, without my telling
them, that he did not believe in having honorary members of college boards of trustees, and as the state of his
health forbade his presence longer at our commencement
exercises, he sent me his resignation as a trustee. How
reluctant the board was to accept it may be known from
the fact that it was laid upon the table and not accepted
until a year after, at his persistent request.

He received his high degree from this college in 1872.
The record in our last Triennial is as follows: Johannes-
Dudley Philbrick, Curator, Dart. 1842 et Mr., Superin-
tentor Bostoniae Scholarum, LL.D.; Univ. Sancti An-
dreae apud Scotos, LL.D., 1878; Officier de l'Instruction
Publique, France, 1878; Chevalier de la Legion d' Hon-
neur, 1878.

The number of men who have done more than John D.
Philbrick to make the world better is small. How sad
that a life such as his was, — so true, so pure, so noble,
so unselfish, — could not have been longer! Yes, it
must be that he is a living, happy man still. I have not
a doubt of it, for, if I doubted it, I should be of all men
most miserable.

" For our citizenship is in heaven, from whence also
we look for the Saviour, the Lord Jesus Christ, who shall
change our vile body that it may be fashioned like unto
his glorious body, according to the working whereby he
is able even to subdue all things unto himself."

LETTER OF HIRAM ORCUTT, LL.D.

John Dudley Philbrick, a classmate in the same section, occupying the same line of seats in the classroom,
and a room only two doors distant, I knew him well ; and
having chosen the same profession, I continued my acquaintance with him to the end.   Many kind, appreciative and tender words have already been spoken of him
since his departure.   I beg to add my tribute of respect
and affection ; for I knew him only to honor, admire, and
love him.

It has been said that Mr. Philbrick was not " a natural
leader in scholarship."   That he was a thorough and successful scholar, his record will show.   That he was " not
brilliant," in the sense this word is generally understood,
may be accounted for by recalling two facts ; viz., his
preparation for college was limited (*only fourteen months
time was allowed him*), and his aim was not to gain the
class leadership and the valedictory, but to acquire a
broader and more practical culture.   Hence, while many
a valedictorian has passed off the stage to be forgotten,
Mr. Philbrick came to the front in his profession, and
not only became a " leader of men," but " of all the men
of the present generation who have devoted their lives
to education, *he was the foremost.*"   This fact, it seems

to me, affords the best possible evidence that he was, after all, a man of "brilliant parts."

It was well said, "-Mr. Philbrick always stood for the right, and standing there he never could be moved." Yes, and he would *fight* for it. With the rowdyism of college life he had no sympathy. An anecdote will illustrate. The self-styled "Dart. Guards," a band of hazers, whose object was to annoy and insult freshmen, came, masked, one evening, into his room. His room-mate hid in the closet, but Mr. Philbrick, armed with a stick of wood, ordered them to leave. Not obeying, he attacked and drove them, sore-headed, from the premises. He had so severely punished them that the organization was never heard from afterward.

That Mr. Philbrick was a true, earnest, and helpful friend, the writer is a grateful witness. Always attentive, kind and sympathetic, he at once gained my confidence and affection, and many times, during our forty years of toil in the same profession, did I seek his counsel and never sought in vain. From no other man have I ever received so much help, encouragement, and inspiration.

But "the great and good man" has gone to his rest,—

"Like one who wraps the drapery of his couch
About him, and lies down to pleasant dreams."

His book of life, as indicated by the magnificent floral book laid upon the foot of his casket by the Boston masters, is "closed," but at least one chapter was unfinished. During my last pleasant interview with Dr. Philbrick, at his home, he told me of his plans and work laid out for the immediate future, and that he was ready to commence it the next morning. He did commence, but could not finish it as he had hoped. Yet "Well done, good and faithful servant," has been spoken, and a monument has been erected to his memory which will never crumble.

LETTER OF H. F. HARRINGTON, A.M.

I heard of the death of Dr. Philbrick with peculiar feelings. I have repeatedly drawn upon his kind friendship for assistance, and it was only a week or two previous to his death that I received from him an extended argumentative letter on a topic of great interest to me. I was preparing an early expression of my gratitude for the benefit it had been when I was saddened by the report that he was no more.

I have known him intimately since the inception of the Centennial Exhibition in Philadelphia, in the Educational Department of which he held a prominent official station. Deputed by him to organize a distinct section of the Massachusetts Exhibit, and repeatedly brought into consultation with him on that and other points connected with the great undertaking, I had ample opportunity to test his powers both as a thinker and an organizer, and I learned to hold him in great respect for his comprehensive grasp of principles, and his sagacious management of affairs.

His services to the cause of education in this country are well known. He was an authority and a power as long as his health enabled him to take an active part in affairs. It can truly be said of him, and it would be a proud record for any man, that there has not been a forward movement in this country in the great cause, which was the paramount joy and interest of his life, with which he was not identified as one of its intelligent instigators and its heartfelt and devoted sponsors. The good he has done is his noblest monument.

LETTER OF A. P. MARBLE, Ph.D.

John D. Philbrick has, for the last quarter of a century, been one of the most conspicuous figures in connection with the American system of common schools. He became superintendent of schools in the city of Boston when that office was yet in its infancy; he was the second incumbent of the office in that city. The organization of the schools in classes, each in a separate room and in care of a separate teacher, was adopted through his influence, in place of the large assembly rooms, with assistant teachers to conduct classes in adjoining recitation rooms, — a plan in vogue generally before this organization. The impetus given to public schools in that city by this organization extended itself to other cities and towns throughout the country. This organization, indeed, has in some instances been carried to excess. no doubt, and there has recently been a healthy reaction, To no one man, perhaps, is due the present advance in education so much as to Mr. Philbrick.

In the exhibits of education at the Centennial in Philadelphia, and at the World's Fair at Paris and at Vienna,

Mr. Philbrick was prominent. He has been influential in bringing this important interest before the public and into a position which its essential character demands. Education is now in the foreground among our national concerns through the life-long activity of Mr. Philbrick. His proud position as an educator places him among our national benefactors, on a line with the statesmen of the land, — the Sumners, the Garfields, and the Manns.

LETTER OF HENRY E. SHEPHERD.

My acquaintance with Dr. Philbrick began during the time that I was Superintendent of Public Instruction, Baltimore, Md., 1875 – 1882. The annual convention of school superintendents, which met usually in Washington, first brought us into personal relations. Our acquaintance soon ripened into a warm friendship, a friendship which, I trust, has not been dissolved, even by death.

> "They do not change who die,
>   Nor lose their mortal sympathy,
>   Nor change to us, although they change."

In conventions and associations in which were embodied the purest and most advanced educational thought of our era, Mr. Philbrick was an acknowledged leader. Indeed, the position seemed to be spontaneously conceded to him; no one .thought of disputing his supremacy. Perfectly devoid of pretentiousness or assumption, somewhat reserved in his bearing toward strangers, he was everywhere recognized, almost intuitively, as an oracle whose utterances upon the grandest educational problems of the time were to be received with profoundest regard and respect. My own opinion is, that the beginning of Mr. Philbrick's *national* renown as a wise and judicious educator, may be traced to the series of Reports issued by him while Superintendent of Public Instruction, Boston, from about 1856 to 1875. The Boston Reports of those years are unsurpassed in modern literature for soundness of judgment, breadth of view, and definiteness of purpose. If collected into a single volume, and published in such form as to be easily available, they would prove invaluable to teachers of all classes throughout our common country. When I first entered upon the delicate and complex duties of Superintendent of Public Instruction in Baltimore, Mr. Philbrick's wise and discriminating Reports were my most trusted guides and counselors. Doubtless scores of others, who never saw his face, can bear testimony similar to my own. The life and work of Mr. Philbrick are a striking refutation of that morbid sentiment which the Poet Laureate has expressed in one of his best-known creations : —

> " The individual withers,
> And the world is more and more."

The colossal results achieved by such men, despite of the most formidable opposition, demonstrate that in no age has the power of individual influence, directed by rational intellect, been more productive and more resistless than in our own.

My last meeting with Mr. Philbrick was in Washington, March, 1882, at the session of our Superintendents' Convention. It was there, if I mistake not, that he read his admirable paper upon the work accomplished by our "city systems," — a paper since issued in its elaborated form by the Department of Education. To those younger than himself, and needing the rare benefits of his matured judgment, he was most kindly and sympathetic. I can never efface the recollection of my last interview with him at the Ebbitt House in Washington, during the session of our convention. How little did I imagine that it was the last!

No man of our generation has surpassed Mr. Philbrick in serene wisdom, discerning judgment, singleness of aim, and continuity of effort. Many of the most excellent characteristics of our school system may be traced to his inspiration; his whole life was a protest against empiricism, mechanism, and all the disingenuous arts by which men of lesser mould have won transient fame.

LETTER OF A. P. STONE, LL.D.

My acquaintance with Mr. Philbrick extended over the whole of his professional life. From the first I was attracted to him as a bright, pleasant man, with winning ways, and an active participant in the early meetings of the Massachusetts Teachers' Association and other gatherings of school workers. On such occasions he was always helpful and inspiring, for he had an intense interest in teachers' meetings, and his professional enthusiasm, which was always of the highest type, gave a kind of glow to his thoughts and words that was peculiarly elevating and enjoyable. As a student of education he was profound in its history, philosophy, and methods. To the progress of the cause of education for the last forty years, and especially in the line of the common schools, he contributed his best thoughts and strength, and with great success.

One of the most noticeable characteristics of Mr. Philbrick was his warm personal interest in his fellow-teachers. For them he always had a pleasant smile of welcome, as well as a word of encouragement and of counsel, if asked for or needed. By his advice to school committees and superintendents, many teachers have found themselves called to improved situations, and oftentimes without ever knowing by whose counsel it was done.

In the death of Mr. Philbrick the cause of education loses one of its most devoted and efficient workers. As a personal friend I feel his loss most keenly.

LETTER OF E. C. CARRIGAN, ESQ.

"We will sell, or deny, or defer right or justice to no man," was a principle of Magna Charta which the barons and the primate of England exacted from an ambitious king. Upon the key-stone of the free, universal education of the people stood John D. Philbrick, foremost among American educators, delaying and denying to none the most liberal tuition offered by a generous public. Whether a child of the city or country, native or foreign born, attending school morning or evening, Mr. Philbrick guarded with watchful, parental care the welfare of every ward of the Commonwealth, encour-

aging all to the highest possible advancement. To him
there were known no boundaries in education, and in
every department of the common school system, at all
times, he insisted that in both day and evening schools
"the best is the best everywhere." Urging this principle, he was practically the sole official promoter, if not
the founder, of our present system of evening schools.
With the yearly influx of foreign population, and the
proneness of parents early to call their children from the
schoolroom to the factory and family support, he claimed
that a well-matured system of evening schools was but
the natural and necessary complement of the day schools.
Instead of committing to the guardianship of an indifferent tax-paying community, he wisely contended for their
establishment under a general mandatory enactment, that
they might be made a permanent part of the State school
system. To this end he most freely gave his voice and
his pen, and added his great influence.

I remember his happy expression and hearty counsel,
when I presented for his criticism the bill then pending
enactment by the legislature of 1883, and which to his
great satisfaction was passed and approved in May of
the same year. Though the act provided for the main-
tenance of evening schools in all cities and towns of ten
thousand and more inhabitants, he still urged the permanent establishment of high schools in larger cities
under the same law.

For evening art and industrial schools he held the
same generous and intelligent views. He thought it important to imitate Great Britain and Continental Europe

in the establishment for artisans and others, evening courses, free to the public, irrespective of sex and occupation. His theory of evening school work was especially practical and wise. He insisted upon close organization and classification, and, like Guizot, believed that "it is the master that makes the school"; that these schools were not designed as an asylum for the superannuated and rejected teachers of day schools, nor to be made the depository of cast-off supplies. On the contrary, he would provide the best accommodations and supplies, and give their management to competent day masters.

In his earliest conception of the design, scope, and management of evening schools, Mr. Philbrick proved himself a wise counsellor ; and in every department, whether advising or supervising, as was said of Wellington, he was something more than a commissary and clerk. He was the founder of principles and originator of methods for these schools, and a master every way competent to direct their use to practical and profitable ends. In criticising a wrong he was ready to suggest the remedy, and his great success in the direction of evening school service was but the legitimate and necessary result of honest, studious, and intelligent effort.

As a friend, a promoter and advocate of secondary instruction in evening schools, his reports offer the best evidence. Of the Boston Evening High School he said, as early as 1874, when it was in charge of Mr. W. Nichols, " I never visited a school in the city that afforded me more satisfaction than this, and in none is the public money expended to better advantage."

Mr. Philbrick's latest encouragement to the mainte-
nance of the school of which he was the 'founder was
probably expressed to a gathering of a few of his personal
friends at the recent reunion of the Franklin School graduates, when, after expressing his great satisfaction at the
establishment of the school in the High and Latin School
building, he said, " Our high schools are the most democratic of all our schools, but the most democratic of high
schools is the evening high school." In his work for this
branch of education his heart was always as generous as
his mind was great. A staunch supporter of the most
liberal appropriations for higher instruction in both day
and evening schools, his counsel and influence were
sought in everything material to the welfare of the evening high school. Of the petitioners who urged the re-
establishment of this school in the high school building,
Mr. Philbrick was among the foremost to champion its
support; and to the day of his death his services were
remembered by the pupils, as expressed in the following
resolutions : —

Whereas, The Boston Evening High School was established
and generously maintained under the direction of Supt. John
D. Philbrick, whose death we regretfully learn :

Resolved, That, by the death of John D. Philbrick, this
school has lost a most constant and faithful friend, whose
labors for evening education were specially marked by zealous,
untiring devotion in all its departments.

Resolved, That, while we, the pupils of the Evening High
School, record our earnest appreciation of his services in our
behalf, we would extend to his bereaved household and
friends our heartfelt sympathy.

Resolved, That a committee of five attend the funeral, and
present to the widow an engrossed copy of these resolutions.

Having resigned his trust, and in every department rendered an account approved by his Commonwealth and country, it was especially fitting that those whom he served with such constant, unselfish devotion should thus record their appreciation of a benefactor and friend, and that we all should pause, if but to consider for a moment the briefest review of the life and labors of one of the greatest savants of his age and the nation's greatest educational public servant.

LETTER OF J. H. HOOSE, Ph.D.

The *Journal* for Feb. 18, 1886, is just at hand. I have read it with peculiar and deep interest. It has been my good fortune to know Mr Philbrick, although not intimately. I remember him with marked pleasure for the interest that he always took in me, — a comparative stranger to him. I remember the deep interest that he took in the tenure of position of teachers. His sympathies were always warm and right. He was, perhaps, the highest type of the practical schoolman, and the most enlightened educator that America has yet produced.

But I write for an additional purpose, which is this : You have devoted one issue of the *Journal* entirely to a memorial of a teacher. This is unprecedented in the history of educational journalism, and it is one of the most thoughtful and praiseworthy acts of these times. The example set by you in this instance will have its influence upon the members of our profession, for it will show to teachers at large that there are many lines of tender memories of teachers which are cherished by the worthy men and women of our fraternity. This memorial will make teachers feel less lonely ; it will strengthen the bonds of brotherhood among them, and help on the era of fraternal sympathy. In honoring the memory of an educator in the manner that you have, you have ennobled the teacher, magnified his profession, and honored educational journalism.

LETTER OF PROF. W. H. PAYNE.

Of the duties binding on men toward their fellows, none is higher or sweeter than that of rendering just praise to those whose forms have forever disappeared from human sight. The tears we shed over the graves of our departed friends are unselfish tributes, pleasing to heaven and wholesome to the soul that weeps. We may thus have the delicious joy of doing a service for which there can be no return ; and by this respite from selfish emotions, the soul gains strength for a new start towards the higher life.

Mr. Philbrick was my dearest professional friend, and his death was a shock whose effects are still vividly felt in my heart. My affection for him was the greater because out of his own generous impulses he bestowed on me his good offices while I was still a stranger to him. Soon after he retired from Boston to Asylum Station, he sent me warm words of commendation for the expression of some sentiment which he approved, and a hearty invitation to visit him whenever my duties might call me to the East. Learning of my contemplated visit to Boston in the winter of 1884-5, he repeated his request for a visit from me, and when I reached my hotel I found a note regretting his inability to meet me in the city, and again urging me to see him at his home. One leading motive for this journey to the East was the pleasure of paying my respects to the friend for whom I had such veneration ; and the moment my immediate duty was done I made my way to Asylum Station. Mr. Philbrick's home was a little way from the station, and his directions had been so minute that I needed no guide to my destination. I was hardly half-way to his house when I was met by a horseman galloping towards the little station. As he came near he seemed to suspect my mission, and in a moment there was mutual recognition. In a few moments more I reached the house, and a hearty welcome by my good hostess was hardly over before Mr. Philbrick returned from his morning gallop to the post-office. I find it impossible to express any adequate notion of my serene enjoyment during the afternoon and evening of that memorable winter's day. I thought then, as I think now, that a more beautiful mode of spending the evening of one's life could hardly be imagined. *Otium cum dignitate* most nearly expresses my impression of Mr. Philbrick's life in the calm retirement of that charming home. The picture of serene and lovable age that is embalmed in the *Cato major*, I seemed to see realized in that New England country seat.

As might be anticipated, our conversations went far into the night and ran chiefly on men and books and institutions as they were related to education and schools. As is well known, Mr. Philbrick had had exceptional advantages for educational observation and study. At Vienna, Paris, and Philadelphia he had employed his time as an expert in the study of education in all its phases, and at the time of his death he was doubtless the wisest public school man in this country. He had gathered books and documents from all the countries he had visited, and his memory was teeming with interesting recollections of the most eminent educators of the world. My professional enthusiasm was rekindled and nourished; and as I bade my good friends adieu on that winter morning, I was grateful to Heaven for such examples of wisdom, goodness, and content as I had seen in that charming home.

In the July following I visited Boston again, and on the morning of the fourth I was again Mr. Philbrick's guest. I met the same hearty greeting as before, and there was a renewal of the same delightful conversations. In the afternoon of that day Mr. Philbrick had his carriage brought to the door and asked me to go out with him for a ride. We drove through shaded lanes for a a few miles, and then into the grounds of a beautiful country residence. Mr. Philbrick presented me to the ladies of the house, and soon after there entered the parlor a plainly dressed man of dignified bearing whom I had observed coming up the lane as we approached the house. Mr. Philbrick had given me the unexpected pleasure of an afternoon call on one of his neighbors, Mr. Whittier.

I dare say Mr. Whittier remembers me, for I did not ask him for his autograph; I have what is better, — a charming mental photograph of the poet, his home, his study, his pet on the porch (a lusty fox squirrel), the conversation on men and books, in which, it seemed to me, that, after all, the man was greater even than the poet; and, finally, the kindly *farewell* as we took our leave.

Our homeward ride took us through Danvers Meadows, and past the old Salem church; and it was twilight when the thread of our conversation was broken by our arrival home.

A few days after I met Mr. Philbrick again at Newport, at the meeting of the American Institute of Instruction; and still later by a few days, at the meeting of the National Association in Saratoga. Finally, I took my leave of him in the parlors of Congress Hall, and was never to see his face again.

INTERNATIONAL TRIBUTE.

In the *Revue Pédagogique*, a monthly educational magazine published in Paris, there appeared, March, 1886, the following appreciative article upon the character and work of Dr. Philbrick. It was written by M. Buisson, a man better qualified than any other in France to estimate Mr. Philbrick's work at its true value, and to do ample justice to his private character. M. Buisson had not only visited the Boston schools, while under Dr. Philbrick's charge, but had often met him at international exhibitions, and had received him into his own home in Paris as a guest, for months during the year of the Paris Exposition. It is no small honor to have won such an opinion from so eminent a scholar and school man as M. Buisson.

JOHN D. PHILBRICK.
(May 27, 1818 — Feb. 2, 1886.)

We cannot let the sad news, brought to us by the *Journal of Education*, of Boston, pass without giving a word of respectful sympathy and homage to the memory of a worthy man, whose loss the United States mourns to-day.

The reputations of teachers and school superintendents rarely cross the ocean from the New World to the Old, or from the Old to the New. The name of Mr. Philbrick has proved one of the first exceptions to this mutual ignorance and indifference. For twenty years his name has been the best known in Europe of all the American educators. And this was only just.

No man has worked more, nor more happily succeeded in making known, in school matters, America to Europeans, or Europe to Americans. He was by his work, his travels, his missions to the great Expositions of Vienna and Paris, his reports, his official publications, the bond of union between two worlds; he was among the first to understand and prove the incomparable advantages of these international relations.

Such a tribute of gratitude as has been rendered to the memory of Mr. Philbrick by his fellow citizens in the United States, is a beautiful end to a man's life. The number of the *Journal of Education* which is consecrated to him forms one of the most touching memorials which could be given to a man to merit. There are in it a series of tender testimonials, all coming from men who have seen him at his work, all full of facts, and of an American directness, without other eloquence than that of personal feeling and sincerity.

One cannot read these pages without seeing how much they honor both the man and the country. A people must be great, free, profoundly republican, and must feel more deeply than trite phrases can express, what education is in the destiny of a country, to give, outside of official recognition, this outpouring of public sympathy, this diversity of admiration, of gratitude, and respect for a man who has been all his life nothing but a school man. A man must be of rare moral worth to have acquired, by such a work, such a popularity. But whoever has known Mr. Philbrick can understand the secret of his power and of his success. He was a spirit upright, guileless, and frank, one of those souls who continue young because they remain sincere. He had found his vocation and he never left it, even in a country and in a time in which men of his ability could find in political life so many more brilliant openings. He never thought of change. He was of those who love teaching, — let us say, rather, let us say as the Americans say, education. He had the happiness to conceive this most beautiful dream and to live it.

When quite young he had heard Horace Mann, and that powerful voice had stirred him even to his inmost soul ; he remembered still, in his last years, some admirable fragments of the lectures of this great patriot, and recited them to us with an emotion that made it impossible not to share in his feeling. Those dying words of Horace Mann had been the motto of his whole life, had sunk into his heart, "Be ashamed to die without having accomplished some victory for humanity."

Through Horace Mann came to him a sort of vision of what a life wholly consecrated to the work of popular education might be. Mr. Philbrick was at that time a simple professor in a small college. He did not dream that for him was reserved the overwhelming task of succeeding Horace Mann, and of being for more than twenty years superintendent of the schools of Boston.

He was still in that position in 1876, at the time of the visit of the French delegates sent to the Centennial Exposition at Philadelphia.

This is not the place to repeat what the delegates said in their joint collective report upon Boston and her schools, the finest, perhaps, in the world. Let us remember that their organization, commenced by Horace Mann, was mostly carried out by the personal work of Mr. Philbrick.

His mind was clear and just, he was always open to ideas of progress. He read or saw all that could in-

struct him, and he borrowed freely from Germany, England, and France all the details of school organization, all
the methods of teaching which seemed to him worthy of
imitation.   But under all the borrowing, there was always
something which was his own, and which gave unity to
his plans, force to his actions, and originality to his
system ; he had an aim and he never lost sight of it, either
in the whole scheme or in the details.   This aim was to
make free citizens for a free country ; it was to give them
education, not from without, but from within ; it was to
reach the life of the soul, and to make education the
apprenticeship of self-government.

How many times in our conversations in Boston,
during our visit, and in Paris during his stay at the
Exposition of 1878, have we noticed with what wonderful
clearness he threw light upon the most delicate and most
complex school questions, by raising himself with a single
bound above secondary interests, to judge and decide
summarily, categorically, in the American fashion,
according to the single criterion, "Is such a practice,
such a method, fit to form freemen ?"   Or again, "If it
is adopted, will our pupils be improved in mind or in
character ? Yes, then it is good. If not, no.

We design at this time neither to undertake the biography of Mr. Philbrick, nor a deep study of his school
work.   But it may be allowed here to reproduce some
lines of his, which will picture him better than any
eulogy.   They are at the end of one of his last reports
to the school committee of Boston ; he is going to resign
his office, and he cannot help reverting to himself at the
moment of bidding a last adieu to his fellow citizens : —

" For upwards of thirty years, — all but four in this city, —
I have occupied, without the intermission of a day, various
positions of service in connection with public schools. Here

my professional career has been run.   It was the career of my choice, and my highest ambition.   My heart has been in it. It has afforded me the desired opportunity for making my humble contribution to the general welfare.   I am thankful for it.   I shall never cease to be grateful to all who have co-operated with me in my efforts to make the Boston Public Schools the best in the world.   And I will venture to say that I ask no ill thing for the cause, when, on parting from this place, I pray that whomsoever you choose to succeed me, he may resemble me in uprightness of intentions and surpass me in abilities."

BOSTON'S TRIBUTE.

BOSTON'S TRIBUTE.

THE MASTERS' ASSOCIATION.

The Boston Masters' Association is composed of all the principals of the Normal, Latin, High, and Grammar Schools, employed in the city of Boston. This Association meets once a month, at the call of the superintendent of schools, for the discussion of educational questions, and for conference in regard to the management of the schools. These meetings are held at the rooms of the school committee, and are followed by a dinner at Parker's.

Here it was that the Boston masters were brought into the most intimate relations with Dr. Philbrick. Here, more than anywhere else, that they learned to appreciate his wisdom, his power in practical affairs, his patience, his thorough appreciation of good work and honest endeavor, and his constant effort to dignify the office of the teacher and make it honorable and desirable. Here, too, it was that the simple honesty of his nature most showed itself, and that warm-hearted generosity which gave due credit to all his co-workers in the cause of education. Here were cemented those bonds of personal friendship which united superintendent and teachers into a band of faithful friends working for the common good of the schools. Here, in short, he learned to respect and love the Boston masters, and here they learned to regard him as the ideal superintendent.

The March meeting of this Association was given up to a commemoration of the work and character of Dr. Philbrick. Among the addresses that evening were the following : —

ADDRESS OF C. GOODWIN CLARK.

Mr. Superintendent and Brother Masters : —

In offering these resolutions for the committee, I wish to add a few personal words of appreciation of the character and characteristics of our beloved and lamented friend.

My acquaintance with Mr. Philbrick began in New Britain, Conn., in the winter of 1852. I had charge of the grammar department of the model school connected with the Normal School, when he was appointed to the principalship, and the following year I became a student of the Normal School, and came daily under his teaching and influence. It has been my good fortune since that time to be on terms of friendship, to go to him for advice, and, for the last twenty-five years, to co-operate with him to do the best thing for the schools of Boston.

His deep personal interest in the students of New Britain attached them to him. He set before them a high ideal, and inspired them with needed confidence. His enthusiasm was contagious, and aroused in them a zeal for improvement and for the doing of worthy work for a noble calling. No matter how short the interview, they left him with enlarged views and nobler aspirations. He was like a charged " Leyden jar " ; whatever teacher came in contact with him received a spark, and he was an unimpressible dullard who was not improved by contact.

I called on him once during a serious illness, when visitors were a hindrance ; but his interest in the work in New Haven, where Prof. Moses True Brown and myself had been sent to do pioneer work in reorganizing the school system of that city, was unabated, and his faithful wife had to check him for exceeding his strength in cheering and counseling us.

Mr. Philbrick had common sense in an uncommon degree, which men call wisdom. He was a needed and appreciated counselor in educational affairs. His growth in wisdom was continuous and symmetrical, like the growth of a tree, and as we who have been long asso- ciated with him have grown in years and experience, we have not outgrown his judgment, but have appreciated it more and more. His consecration to education was com- plete. In him was illustrated the saying of the Great Teacher, " If thine eye be single thy whole body shall be full of light."

It is human for ignorance and inexperience to speak lightly and perhaps disparagingly of our official supe- riors, whom we do not know or cannot appreciate. I have heard such remarks regarding Mr. Philbrick, and it has been interesting to note the changed opinions of such when placed in responsible positions. " I did not appreciate Mr. Philbrick until I came to this responsibility," has been the usual remark.

Mr. Philbrick had a cheerful theory for earnest, ambitious young men ; it was that whatever happened was for the best, and that the lesson they were to learn was "to labor and to wait." There are those present to whom his words were the silver lining to their cloud of disappointment.

It has been said by one who knew him most intimately, that he "idealized his *friends.*" I think the charge is true, and am sure that he often embarrassed them by his opinion of what they were capable of doing, and his earnestness to have them do it. What a tribute to his generous heart that he "idealized his friends" and thought them capable of doing things beyond their own estimate ! How many of us think more highly of our friends than we ought to think ? Yes, there was nothing disparaging in Mr. Philbrick's nature. He saw the best in every school, in every teacher, in every school official ; he saw merit from afar.

His charity was Christ-like. "They know not what they do," was his feeling toward ignorant and wrong-headed officials, for whom he never seemed to entertain bitterness or ill-nature, though they would have overturned the slow progress of years, and illustrated the saying of Goethe, "There is nothing so terrible as active ignorance."

I once called on Mr. Philbrick at his office, and he told me that he had just written a letter of sympathy to a member of the school committee, then in his last illness, who, for a quarter of a century, had opposed all his recommendations, disparaged his labors, and seemed to delight in keeping things as they were. I said, "How could you do it?" He replied, with tenderness, "I couldn't help it; I never laid up anything against him. He never understood me."

Mr. Philbrick was fortunate in his time of coming to Boston. There was a great work to be done in harmonizing and systematizing the educational work, and in reconstructing the primary schools in accordance with modern ideas and methods; work that once done wisely needs not to be done again. How patiently, persistently, and wisely he labored, with no assistant, not even a clerk, you, senior Masters, well know, and with what success all well-informed educators also know. This leavening of the schools was accomplished without the authority to appoint or remove a single teacher. It was like the genial influence of the sun on the vegetable world.

He was fortunate in his last visit to Europe, after his work in Boston was done, and his able reports had been read abroad, and given reputation to the Boston schools.

The congress of educators from the chief countries of Europe, after such an acquaintance as long service on important juries and committees afforded, paid him honor and deference. His genial spirit and courtly manners, united with wide knowledge and wisdom in counsel, won the affection and esteem of his associates. Educational men traveling in Europe afterwards found Mr. Philbrick the most honored educational man in America.

As highest summits are first seen from afar, he

returned from Europe with the reputation of a leader and an authority in educational affairs.

Mr. Philbrick was fortunate in his domestic relations ; his devoted wife was a hearty co-worker in his plans. She was an ideal companion in her hospitality to his friends, and in her sympathy with his aspirations. His domestic life was congenial to his heart and stimulating to his ambition.

Mr. Philbrick was not blessed with children, but he gave his life to educate the children of others. He took the children of Boston in his arms and blessed them. Let us, above all men, speak his name with loyalty to his memory, with gratitude for his great service, with reverence and admiration for his character, and affectionate remembrance of his friendship.

Let us ask that a noble schoolhouse be named for him who did so much for Boston schools.

ADDRESS OF ROBERT SWAN.

Mr. Superintendent and Brethren : —

It was not my privilege to enjoy intimate personal relations with Dr. Philbrick, but it was my privilege to be the master of a school during the whole time of his administration of the office of superintendent ; and I can certify without bias to the manner in which his duties were performed.

My first knowledge of Mr. Philbrick was at the time of his appointment as writing-master of the Mayhew School, forty years ago. The schools were then on the old system, so called, each with a grammar and a writing master, the scholars alternating, morning and afternoon. My brother, William D. Swan, was master in the Grammar Department, and, consequently, I was fully informed in regard to the enthusiasm and ability with which Mr. Philbrick discharged the duties of his position. There were two large halls, in each of which there were four teachers and two hundred boys, the master at one end of the room, an usher at the other, with two female teachers between them, who retired with half a class at a time to recitation rooms. What a school of experience for a young master!

His success here pointed to him, emphatically, as the man to take charge of the new Quincy school, the building for which was then in progress of erection, and he was transferred to this position, leaving the Mayhew with Mr. Swan as sole master, and inaugurating the Quincy with single classrooms, on the new system with a single head. There is no need of reciting the story of his great success in the new school. The two schools were so conducted that the old system, though strenuously supported by its advocates, was abandoned, and the new order became general, and is in vogue at the present time.

The next step in progress in the school system was the permission from the legislature for the city to appoint a superintendent of schools, and Mr. Philbrick was a prominent candidate for the place. Mr. Bishop, who had been, for some time previous, superintendent of the Providence schools, was chosen, and Mr. Philbrick soon after resigned his mastership in Boston to take charge of a

normal school in Connecticut. The gentleman opposite
has spoken of the good fortune that always attended
Mr. Philbrick, and we can now appreciate how fortunate
he was in not succeeding in his first application for the
position of superintendent, for the experience in Connecticut was absolutely necessary to properly prepare him
for his great work, which he afterward so successfully
matured, of perfecting a school system for Boston.

Mr. Bishop soon resigned, and Mr. Philbrick was then
appointed without opposition. When he commenced his
duties, the Grammar and Primary School committees
were entirely separate organizations, the Primary Committee being chosen by the Grammar Board from names sent
in to them by individuals who were willing to serve in
that capacity. Each primary schoolroom contained all
the classes of the primary grade. The law was changed,
bringing all the schools under one Board, and, later, the
schools were organized in groups of six classes, each class
in a separate room. Then came the placing of the primary schools under the supervision of the masters of the
districts, thus making a systematic grading from the
child's entering the schools, at five years of age, till the
graduation from the grammar school at fifteen. The
magnitude of this improvement, in accomplishing which
Mr. Philbrick was the leading, directing spirit, those
listening to me can fully appreciate.

Mr. Philbrick's influence was powerful in advancing
the status of the teacher's calling in the estimation of
the public, and in thus increasing their compensation.
The salaries in many instances are now double what were

paid in 1857, calling in superior service, and attaching men to the occupation for life, rather than, as was too often the case in former times, making teaching a temporary expedient to provide the means to pursue some one of the professions.

I might enumerate the judicious programme prepared for the schools, the establishment of the Normal School for girls, the advancement of industrial work, now so popular but in former years lacking support among educators, and other elements of progress all around us, but the minds of most present are too familiar with his later work to make such enumeration in this presence necessary. Our thoughts at this time turn to him as the leading educator among the many noble men who have labored among us.

Dr. Philbrick was considered by some a timid man, but what was thought timidity was only extreme carefulness. He fully surveyed the whole field before making any important change, and his sagacity was such that, throughout his whole term of service, there was constant progress. There was never at any time a necessity for taking any step backwards.

Words of eulogy are too often exaggerated, and awaken in those who hear them painful comparison with the person's actual character; but to-night no sentiment of the kind suggests itself to any one present. We have listened to words truthful and sincere, bearing the corresponding impress from the depths of feeling. If any other token of the estimation in which our departed friend was held was necessary, the throng of men, educators from various parts of the state, who braved the most inclement day of the winter to stand sorrowing about his body in the beautiful home made desolate by his death, would attest the love and esteem in which he was held by those who had known him longest and best.

ADDRESS OF JOSHUA BATES, LL. D.

Mr. Chairman and Gentlemen of the Masters' Association:

I desire on this occasion to add my testimony to the many expressions of regard which have already been uttered in appreciation of our departed friend, the Hon. John D. Philbrick.

Born in the Granite State, of worthy parentage, Dr. Philbrick, amidst comfortable surroundings, was trained by the circumstances of his early life to habits of industry, and patient labor. He early learned that success in life could be secured only by personal effort and close application to all duties. It is a prominent characteristic of our republican institutions that many a boy early learns that he must depend on his own resources, often under almost insurmountable difficulties, in order to reach positions of usefulness and honor.

In the school, academy, and college, we find young Philbrick the vigorous boy, the industrious young man, assiduously devoting his time and talents to the faithful performance of all requirements.

Early in life, he made the decision to devote his energies to the profession of teaching. He was not, perhaps, what could be called a genius; yet his application was so untiring that he accomplished by industry what genius often fails to do. He had unlimited influence with his classmates, and was thoroughly appreciated and respected by all the college officers.

Success in discipline and instruction in his first school experiences, led him soon to find and secure positions that developed great executive ability in all educational organization and administration. Blest in youth with robust health and a mind acute and vigorous, with a keen sense of moral rectitude, we find Dr. Philbrick in his manhood equipped and ready for all undertakings, however laborious and difficult. His character was remarkable for strong common sense, symmetry, and completeness. He had a clear, intuitive insight into the character of men, as well as the relation and fitness of things. He exhibited, in a remarkable degree, kindness of heart and gentleness of spirit, but also uncommon strength of purpose. His social qualities were of a high order ; he was always cheerful and affable, which, with a cultivated intellect and courteous manner, made him the most delightful of companions. He acquired knowledge by constant study and retained it with great tenacity, and was able to apply it with skill and efficiency. His perceptive faculties were quick and his memory ready and retentive, so that in company, at home, and in his travels, he was at school, gathering knowledge for future use. He kindly sympathized with all teachers desirous to do their duty, and aided them in all their trials by judicious encouragement and advice.

My acquaintance with Dr. Philbrick dates from the year 1844, while he was connected as usher with the

English High School. On the organization of the Quincy
School in 1848, and the appointment of Dr. Philbrick as
its master, I soon learned the worth and value of his com-
panionship. Owing to the proximity of the Quincy and
Brimmer districts, we naturally had occasion to consult
on matters pertaining to our respective schools, and
thus we became quite intimate. Such was the harmony
of our views on all educational subjects, that our hitherto
casual meetings were changed to frequent interviews, that
ripened into mutual and warm friendship, which continued uninterrupted to the last.

I propose to speak briefly of Dr. Philbrick, as some of
this association of masters knew him in years past in
friendly and professional intercourse, calling up in pleasing reminiscences some characteristics familiar to those
of us who were associated with him in social life and in
educational work.

The social element in his character and his genial
nature were such as to gather around him a host of
friends ; and the quiet but sterling integrity of the man
created confidence in all who secured his friendship.
Any one at all acquainted with our friend must have particularly noticed his calm demeanor, fortitude, and noble
bearing under all circumstances, either of success or dis-
couragement, in his professional life. Dr. Philbrick's
character never shone brighter than when he was surrounded by difficulties and trials. Such firmness and
dignity, such undisturbed peace of mind, such conscious-
ness of no wrong-doing, — for his natural frankness forbade all duplicity, — and such manly and Christian resig-

nation gave a peculiar loveliness to the man, and all his friends admired his noble bearing under all trials and oppositions.

Dr. Philbrick, after carefully and thoroughly investigating any subject, and becoming convinced what course, in his best judgment, was the proper and honest one to pursue, held fast and firmly to his convictions, and was decided and independent in action. He was emphatically practical and sound in all educational opinions. He was distinguished for completeness in mental endowments, and was so well stocked with good common sense that he could not brook or sustain any sensational or empirical notions in any department of his work ; but he was never rude or offensive in his opposition to what he considered unsound and visionary theories. He labored constantly and aimed conscientiously to encourage and sustain all methods in discipline and teaching that would lead to thorough instruction and complete scholarship. He so heartily and truly desired substantial and definite results, that he totally ignored all shams and all desultory and uncertain methods. He was far more willing to submit peaceably to defeat, than ignobly to compromise, or substitute any system that would encourage superficial teaching and the fanciful schemes of modern agitators. In this particular he ranks pre-eminent for honesty and unflinching purpose in all undertakings. While some constantly cater for public approbation, and shift and turn to gain applause, he was ever truly and perseveringly committed to such methods as would conduce to practical and genuine results.

In his domestic, social, and public life we know his worth, as an affectionate husband, a faithful brother teacher, and more recently as a wise, conservative, and judicious superintendent and director of all school administrations; we well know how earnestly and independently he devoted himself to duty, and the deep interest he ever felt in all teachers and their profession; and how kindly and patiently he always listened to any suggestions and inquiries, and never in an authoritative manner forced his opinions on any one.

Dr. Philbrick will ever hold a high rank as a clear and vigorous interpreter of the best educational methods. He wrote from the amplest intellectual resources and from deliberate thought. He had the rarest opportunities, both in this country and abroad, and by study and personal observation he became familiar with various systems in education, and learned to utilize philosophical deductions therefrom, so that he may justly be ranked among the foremost exponents of pedagogical science in the world.

His reports, lectures, and essays on various subjects of school interest and importance are prolific and thorough, and designate him as the highest authority in all questions of popular education. His series of school reports, as superintendent of the Boston schools, will ever be prized for the great amount of sound, practical information they contain, and as highly important contributions to school literature. His recent admirable circular of the Bureau of Education, Washington, D. C., entitled, " City School Systems of the United States," may justly be considered almost unrivalled, as the ablest and fullest document on educational matters, that has yet been issued from the American press ; thorough, profound, and completely covering all the ground in educational investigation. The wide range of topics so ably considered and analyzed, and the rare power of observation brought to bear on all subjects of organization and methods of instruction, for city schools especially, give the entire report a remarkable interest, and assign the author a prominent place in educational science.

Dr. Philbrick expressed the hope, if health and strength permitted, to write the History of American Education. He was engaged at the time of his death on some important papers ; and it is to be hoped he has left complete additions to his already valuable publications. Says the poet Whittier, for many years the friend and neighbor of Dr. Philbrick, "He leaves a noble record, and his name will long be cherished as a wise and successful friend of learning, and as a worthy and upright citizen"; and his friend, General Eaton, recently United States Commissioner of Education, bears this testimony to his work : "An able, scholarly, and noble man, dear friend, great educator, full of knowledge, wise to plan and faithful to execute, his death is a calamity to sound learning the world over." What higher eulogiums could be engraven on the monument of any man, than such praise, emanating from men ranking high in literary attainment and scholarship.

Dr. Philbrick always took a deep interest in this Association, believing in a full and free discussion of all

subjects pertaining to the best welfare of the schools.
As a presiding officer, he presented his views with
clearness and sincerity. He never in a dictatorial or
offensive manner urged the adoption of any measure,
but waited patiently till all became satisfied that his
suggestions and recommendations would conduce to the
best interests of the schools.

The important lesson to be drawn from such a life of
upright and independent action as vitalized the whole
being of Dr. Philbrick, should create an anxious desire,
especially in teachers, to foster and develop those leading
and prominent characteristics which gave a peculiar
charm to his public and official life.   His defence of
truth and honest opinion was a marked feature in the
career of this noble man, and this should be cherished
and remembered of him, as it is the key-stone of all that
is lofty in character, and the most fitting armor for the
greatest in this world's arena; and it should be the constant aim of all to cultivate and unfold in their teaching
that independence and conscientiousness which prepare
the opening and receptive minds of the young for stations
of influence and honor in life's career.

The name of the departed will still live in all its
blessed influence, not only in the hearts of a multitude
of friends, but also in most grateful recognition by all
who can appreciate his noble work and the vast amount
of good accomplished by him in his industrious life.

Says Pericles, the Grecian statesman, " The earth is
the sepulchre of illustrious men ; nor is it the inscription
on their monuments alone that shows their worth, but the

unwritten memorial of them in remembrance." So we, my brethren, may never stand by the grave, or read the epitaph of him we all so mourn, but we shall often recall his many virtues and dwell with satisfaction and profit on the noble record of a life so active, so useful, and so honorable.

At the close of these addresses the following resolutions, offered by a committee appointed at the previous meeting of the Association, consisting of C. Goodwin Clark, W. E. Eaton, James F. Blackinton, Elbridge Smith, and Granville B. Putnam, were unanimously adopted, and the meeting adjourned : —

RESOLUTIONS.

The masters of the public schools of Boston hereby express their sense of personal bereavement at the great loss they and the cause of education have sustained in the death of John D. Philbrick, who for twenty years was superintendent of the public schools of this city.

He was great as an organizer and masterly in execution. To his devotion, wisdom, enthusiasm, and wise conservatism, the excellence of our schools to-day is, in large measure, due.

His forty-five reports to the school committee are valuable contributions to education. They are notable for sound judgment, wise suggestions, and statesman-like sagacity. They have given an educational reputation to Boston at home and in foreign countries.

We lament the loss of a noble man and a sincere friend, whose wise counsel was always at our command, whose kindly sympathy encouraged and strengthened us in trouble, whose enthusiasm was contagious, whose cheerfulness was perennial, whose patience was unwearied, and whose charity extended to all, even to those who could not understand his motives or appreciate his labors.

While we bow in submission to the will of an all-wise and loving Father, we confess our disappointment that his life was not prolonged to serve still further the cause which he loved, and for which freedom from public duties had furnished the opportunity, and his ripened wisdom had so eminently fitted him.

May his elevated character, his devotion to the cause of popular education, and his love for those who labor in it be to us an example and an inspiration.

THE SCHOOLMASTERS' CLUB.

The Schoolmasters' Club is a social and professional club, composed of teachers, superintendents, editors of educational journals, and other school men of New England, who dine together several times each year, and discuss educational questions. Dr. Philbrick was one of the original members of the New England Pedagogical Society, from which the Schoolmasters' Club sprang. He had always retained his membership in the club, — indeed had been made an honorary member.

At a meeting of this club, held Feb. 20, 1887, addresses were made as follows, in support of resolutions read by Larkin Dunton : —

ADDRESS OF JAMES F. BLACKINTON.

Among those who have taken a prominent part in educational affairs in our day, the name of John D. Philbrick stands in the foremost rank. During his career in this city, some of us, members of this Association, were witnesses of his course from the beginning, from his position as assistant teacher to his crowning work, the re-organization and successful management of the Boston schools. We saw his untiring industry, his persistent purpose, his calm patience under opposition and provocation, and when the triumph came, we saw how meekly and gracefully he bore his honors.

One of the strong points in Mr. Philbrick's character was the rare judgment he showed in steering between extreme educational conservatives on the one side, and violent radicals on the other. He had a profound distrust of all educational hobbies. Always ready to examine what was new and promised to be valuable, he pursued the even tenor of his way, refusing to be turned aside from his purpose by any patent devices or short cuts to educational success.

Another of his peculiar traits, as I knew him, was his desire to find out the best side of every teacher's character. Too many of us, I fear, who have the supervision of teachers, seem to regard criticism as the principal function of our office. We seem to think if we find the bad, the good will take care of itself. This was not Mr. Philbrick's method. He first carefully sought and commended all that was excellent in a teacher's work, and then, in the kindest manner, pointed out what needed correction. This was one thing that gave him so strong a hold on the love and respect of the teachers of Boston. As the years go by, I believe the work of Mr. Philbrick in all departments, as teacher, superintendent, and writer, will be more and more appreciated, and the conviction will be strengthened that this work will bear the test of near approach and strict examination.

But we are told that Mr. Philbrick was not a great man. No, as the term is generally understood, perhaps not. What is a great man? I once heard Mr. Everett say, a great man is one who sets his mark on the institutions of his age, and leaves the world better for his having lived. John Dudley Philbrick set his mark on the educational institutions of Boston, and left them better than he found them.

It has been said within the last few weeks that Mr. Philbrick's death was untimely. So it was when we remember what was expected of him. When he left us here in Boston, we had a right to look for ten or fifteen years more of active educational work from him. But when we look at what he did, his death was not untimely. He accomplished more in that fifty years than others would have accomplished in a century. So far as the true purposes of living and doing for his fellowmen are concerned, the span of a patriarch's life was but a fraction compared with that threescore years and nearly ten, so nobly and so grandly filled. As we said a few months ago of one of our departed members, we look with just pride and satisfaction on the record of a full and rounded life, devoted, for half a century, to the noble cause that lay nearest his heart.

ADDRESS OF GRANVILLE B. PUTNAM.

Mr. President and Gentlemen: —

As I have known our friend, Mr. Philbrick, longer, and, in some respects, more intimately than any other one present, I desire to say a few words upon this occasion. As you know, he was born in Deerfield, N. H., and this home of his childhood was ever dear to him. Until the time of his death he retained the old homestead in his possession, and it was his delight to revisit it. Every rock and tree was a familiar friend. To trim these trees seemed almost a passion, and he took great pride in their growth and symmetrical development under his pruning hand. He often spoke in admiration of the scenery, which was so rugged and picturesque, and predicted that the time would come when Deerfield would be a favorite place of summer resort.

His father was a man of strong character, whom he much resembled. As he lay upon his death-bed, a likeness of his father was placed in my hand, and as I looked from one to the other, I was struck with the marked resemblance.

He spent his time much as country boys do, attending school during short terms, making maple sugar, breaking steers, etc. He was a young man of courage and muscle, and I have often heard him tell the story of the reception he gave the sophomores who visited his room early in his freshman year. Instead of complying with their demands, he seized a chair and with a tiger-like strength and agility drove them not only from the room but down the stairs. He was soon summoned to the study of the President. He went with a good deal of trepidation, told his story, and waited for his sentence. The President slowly said, " Freshman Philbrick, you did just right, just right. You can go, sir."

My personal knowledge of Mr. Philbrick dates back to

the year 1839, I think, when he was a student in Dartmouth College. Having had a little experience in teaching, he resolved to secure a winter school in Massachusetts, and fixed upon $20 per month as his price. He started out on foot, traveling from town to town, seeking a situation in the town of Danvers, until he reached a schoolhouse painted white, with green blinds. This structure seemed to him palatial, and he decided that if he could secure a position there he would teach for $19 per month.

My father was Prudential Committeeman that year, and young Philbrick sought him out and presented his application. He was taken out upon a bridge leading from the shoe factory to the storehouse for a private consultation. The bridge was in plain view from a kitchen window, where were grouped the young ladies of the family, who indulged in remarks at the expense of his personal appearance. Foremost among these was my aunt, who afterwards became his devoted wife. His was the first winter school which I attended.

In the spring of 1849 I came to Boston, and was again his pupil, having entered the first class in the Quincy School. This was soon after its establishment upon the single-headed plan. Mr. Philbrick was its first master, and fully believing in this plan of organization, he entered with all the energy of his nature upon the task of making it a success. He was rewarded by being permitted to see this plan, together with that of having a single room for each teacher and a single desk for each pupil, adopted in every portion of the land.

This was the first school to be furnished with a large
assembly hall.   In this he was accustomed to have public
exercises.   These were very fully attended, and aided in
increasing the fame of the school.   His discipline was
firm, and upon frequent occasions he vigorously applied
the rod, as I can testify from personal experience.   I
should, however, consider his government mild for those
days.

Mr. Philbrick was a man of scholastic tastes, and a
hard student.   Mr. Wm. H. Leonard, for many years his
next-door neighbor, once told me that when awake he
could always tell the midnight hour by hearing him split-
ting his wood for the morning fire ; for this he always
did when his evening work in the study was ended.   Mr.
Philbrick possessed a great store of educational facts, and
had them at his command, so that he was, in my opinion,
better equipped for writing the history of Education in
America than any other man.   This would have been
for him a noble task, but if ever written it must be by
another hand.

I must not occupy your time longer, but I would bear
witness to his nobleness of character and usefulness to
men.   His manner was so simple and unassuming that
some said he was not a great man ; but if the standard
which Brother Blackinton has suggested is the true
one, — namely, that he is great who leaves his mark
upon his age, surely John Dudley Philbrick was a
great man.

RESOLUTIONS.

The following resolutions were then unanimously adopted, and a copy ordered to be engrossed and sent to Mrs. Philbrick : —

Resolved, That the Schoolmasters' Club of Boston desire to place on record the following statement of their appreciation of the life and services of their late beloved associate, Dr. John D. Philbrick : —

He was a man of eminent ability. No one talent, indeed, over-shadowed all the rest; but his mind, well-rounded and evenly balanced, was one of remarkable force.

He had great power of application. From the beginning of his college course, almost to the day of his death, he was an incessant worker. For him no pains was too great, and no needed labor was too severe.

His life was given to the cause of education. His profession was chosen as early as his sophomore year in college, and seems to have been followed with his whole soul to the very end. In his view it was a high and holy calling, and worthy of the highest ambition of the noblest minds.

He studied education from the standpoint of history and philosophy. No man of the age in which he lived was better acquainted with the history of school systems, educational theories, and methods of teaching. His very conservatism resulted from his knowledge of limitations.

His integrity never faltered. Honesty, both intellectual and moral, was a native element in his character. Selfish aims and ambitions found no lodgment in his heart. He preferred failure to insincerity.

He was generous and sympathetic. No man was quicker to detect merit in others, or more ready to give credit where it was due. Thousands of teachers have been cheered by his kind words of sympathy and wise counsel. He was a friend to all who were honestly working for the good of public schools.

Patient toward those who differed from him in opinion, he was possessed of the true Christian spirit of forgiveness toward his enemies. His later life was a constant exhibition of his conviction that it is better to suffer wrong than to do wrong. It was impossible to provoke him to the doing of an impolite act or the saying of an impolite word.

His life has been a grand success. Wherever public schools exist his influence is felt, and will long continue to be felt, for good. His mind was clear and strong; his character was round and full and sweet; and his life contributed in no small measure to the well being of the world in which he lived.

May we cherish his memory and emulate his example.

THE SCHOOL COMMITTEE.

The following resolutions were offered at a meeting of the School Committee of Boston, February 9, 1886, by William C. Williamson, a member who had served on the old board of school committee, while Dr. Philbrick was superintendent. The resolutions were unanimously adopted by a rising vote : —

Resolved, That the School Committee desire to place on record their deep and abiding sense of gratitude for the long and eminent service rendered in the cause of public education by John D. Philbrick, lately deceased. For twenty years he was superintendent of our schools. During that period his efforts were constant and untiring to enlarge their usefulness and powers, to raise their standard, and to keep them fully up to the requirements of advanced intelligence, and he left them in a better condition than when he entered upon his office, by reason of his labor, watchfulness, and forethought. He was in his profession an idealist, an enthusiast. " He was a scholar, and a ripe and good one, exceeding wise, fair-spoken, and persuading"; but he was also a conservative, not too easily convinced of the soundness of new fashions in education ; gifted with executive and practical skill, and with a personal influence which made him known throughout the schools. In his forty-five printed reports he has placed upon the files of this committee a lasting memorial of his learning, his good sense, and his sanguine hopes. These, with their wise suggestions drawn from his experience and observation of the progress of education at home and in foreign countries, will afford light upon many questions, and bear fruitful testimony to his ability and character for many years to come.

PUBLIC MEMORIAL SERVICES.

At a meeting of the Boston Masters' Association, held March 2, 1886, a committee, consisting of Robert Swan, of the Winthrop School, Moses Merrill, Ph.D., of the Latin School, Larkin Dunton, LL.D., of the Normal School, C. Goodwin Clark, of the Gaston School, and George R. Marble, of the Chapman School, was appointed to arrange for holding a public memorial service in Boston, sometime the following autumn, in honor of Dr. John D. Philbrick.

This committee decided to invite Gilman H. Tucker of New York, Larkin Dunton of Boston, and Dr. Wm. T. Harris of Concord, Mass., to address the friends of the honored dead, at a meeting to be held the following autumn. All these gentlemen accepted the invitation.

The meeting was held, November 5, 1886, in the spacious hall of the Public Latin School building, on Warren avenue, Boston. The public schools of the city were dismissed on the occasion. Mr. Edwin P. Seaver, Superintendent of Schools, presided. The hall was crowded with teachers, past and present members of the Boston School Committee, and other school men. The widow of the lamented dead and a large circle of intimate friends occupied seats reserved for them. Prayer was offered by Granville B. Putnam of the Franklin School. Mr. Seaver, on taking the chair, spoke as follows : —

ADDRESS OF HON. EDWIN P. SEAVER.

Ladies and Gentlemen : —

We have met to-day, that we may testify our respect for the memory of one, the record of whose life-work fills a large place in the educational history of Boston, — John Dudley Philbrick. If one were to begin with the benefits of a mere physical or material kind for which the cause of education is indebted to Mr. Philbrick, there would be much to say of the convenient, cheerful, often beautiful schoolhouses, which adorn all parts of our city ; but it is enough now to remember that the crowning glory of them all, — this palatial building in which we are now assembled, — is due more to his efforts than to those of any other one man. And yet benefits of this kind are among the least of his claims to remembrance. The visitor to St. Paul's Cathedral, in London, is reminded, by the inscription he reads over the tomb of Sir Christopher Wren, that if he would behold the great architect's monument he must look about him. But he who may hereafter look for Mr. Philbrick's monument will find it not in marble tablet or granite shaft that may mark his grave near

his country home, nor even in the palatial schoolhouses
raised during his long administration, all around us,
but in the common school system itself of the city of
Boston, — and in the vast influence which, through that
system, he has exerted upon schools and scholars throughout this land.

The three characteristics of Mr. Philbrick which
have impressed me most were his sound, practical
wisdom, his steadfastness or courage in defence of his
opinions, and his ardent professional enthusiasm.   In
his earlier years he was a reformer, and these characteristics made him successful.   Later in life his
position was more conservative ; not, however, because
he had surrendered his cherished convictions, or abated
his enthusiasm, but rather because the later advances in
educational methods were not fully trusted by him.

But others will speak of his character more fully
than I have a right to speak now.   It is for me to intro-
duce to you speakers who have known him long and
loved him well.   Let me add but one word more.   We
say we have assembled to do honor to Mr. Philbrick's
memory.   How shall we truly do that ?   If all wish to
honor his memory sincerely, — in the manner in which
he would most approve, — we shall carry some of the
inspiration of this hour into our daily duties, and ded-
icate ourselves anew to all that is high and noble in
the great work which he loved so well.

The Superintendent then introduced the speakers
whose addresses form the first three chapters of this

volume, and at the close of the speaking read the following letter from R. Kuki, the Japanese Minister to
the United States : —

LETTER OF THE JAPANESE MINISTER.

WASHINGTON, D. C., Nov. 3d, 1886.

Gentlemen : —

Although unavoidably prevented, to my
great regret, from being with you in person, I desire
most sincerely to join with you in doing honor to the
memory of that very distinguished man, the late John
D. Philbrick, whose benevolent labors have been productive of so much good, not only in the United States
of America, but all over the world. I first had the
pleasure of being associated with him in 1878, at the
Universal Exposition at Paris, where both of us were
appointed " *Membres de Juries* " on the subject of
education. I found him to be a gentleman who won
universal respect, not only as a savant, but also on
account of his attractive manners. I was one of many
who became warmly attached to him, and derived great
benefit from my intercourse with him, particularly in our
conversations on topics connected with education. I
shall never cease to cherish, with the most profound
respect, the memory of our friendship and of his thorough knowledge and excellent judgment, as well as his
eminently admirable character. With the assurance of
my sincere sympathy with you on this occasion, believe
me to remain,

With great respect,

Yours faithfully,

R. KUKI,

His Imperial Japanese Majesty's
Envoy Extraordinary and Minister Plenipotentiary.

MISCELLANEOUS RESOLUTIONS.

Miscellaneous Resolutions.

The following resolutions, adopted by various associations and communities in different parts of the country will show something of the extent and strength of Dr. Philbrick's influence throughout the nation : —

DEPARTMENT OF SUPERINTENDENCE OF THE NATIONAL EDUCATIONAL ASSOCIATION.

ALLIANCE, OHIO, March 15, 1886.

Mrs. John D. Philbrick, Danvers, Mass.,

DEAR MADAM : — At the late meeting of the Department of Superintendence of the National Educational Association at Washington, D. C., the following resolutions were unanimously adopted : —

Whereas, We, the officers and members of the Department of Superintendence of the National Educational Association, have learned of the death of John Dudley Philbrick, LL.D., of Massachusetts, who for more than twenty-five years has been an active and enthusiastic member and an ex-President of the Association, desiring to place upon record our appreciation, esteem, and love of him, adopt the following : —

Resolved, That this Association mourns the loss of one of its most devoted and intelligent workers in the

cause of popular education. As a teacher, superintendent, and writer upon educational topics for more
than a third of a century, he has ranked among the
foremost educators of this country. Wise and discreet
in counsel, energetic and enthusiastic in action, helpful
and sympathetic in his relations with his co-workers,
he left behind him a record full of inspiration and
worthy of imitation.

Resolved, That the cause of general education has
sustained a heavy loss in being deprived of his zeal,
energy, and wisdom, which have pre-eminently characterized his long career.

Resolved, That the Department of Superintendence
especially desires to recognize the eminent services of
Mr. Philbrick in this special field of educational work,
in which he labored nearly a quarter of a century,
achieving not only a national, but a world-wide reputation as a superintendent of instruction.

Resolved, That these resolutions be entered upon the
minutes of this department, and that a copy of them be
sent to Mrs. Philbrick, to whom we tender our sincere
sympathy in her great bereavement.

W. E. SHELDON,
A. J. RICKOFF,   } *Com.*
R. W. STEVENSON, }

CHARLES C. DAVIDSON,
    Sec. Dep't of Superintendence.

TRUSTEES OF THE PHILBRICK-JAMES LIBRARY.

The trustees of the Philbrick-James Library, having
learned with deep regret of the death of Hon. John D.
Philbrick, desire to place on record their appreciation of
his worth as a man, of his long and successful labor as an

educator, and especially of his interest in, and his services for the Philbrick-James Library.

Personally and as a Board we lament the loss sustained by his native town and by the Library which bears his name. His interest in both was great, and the aid rendered in selecting the Library was invaluable.

His thorough knowledge of the wants of the community and his intimate acquaintance with books enabled him to make the Library of the greatest possible value.

We express our sense of the salutary influence the Library has exerted, and feel that in it Mr. Philbrick has a memorial in the contemplation of which his friends may well be gratified.

We extend to his widow our sympathy in her great sorrow, and have instructed our Secretary to forward to her and to place on our records this expression of our appreciation of Dr. Philbrick's worth, and the greatness of his love.

Deerfield, N. H., March 4, 1886.

TEACHERS OF DENVER.

The following communication to the *Journal of Education* will explain itself :—

Dear Sir: — I could write a volume without exhausting the expression of my admiration and love for the life and work of Dr. Philbrick. But you have no room, and I lack ability. Herewith please find an expression of my associates.

Very respectfully,   AARON GOVE.

At the meeting of the teachers of District No. 1, after the superintendent had announced by appropriate remarks the death of Dr. Philbrick, at his home at Asylum

Station, Massachusetts, a committee, representing the three several departments, — primary, grammar, and high schools, — was appointed to prepare fitting resolutions of respect.

The Committee prepared the following, which were adopted : —

With the death of John D. Philbrick, we realize the loss to the profession of one of the ablest, truest, and noblest of schoolmasters ; of a life devoted to the interests of public education, stopped in the midst of its best efforts.

Along with the thousand other tributes that will be presented, the teachers of Denver beg leave to submit, in token of their respect to his memory, an expression of their kind remembrance of his life and works, and of their high appreciation of the magnitude and value of his career to the school world of America and Europe, and offer the prayer that many teachers of this land may follow in the footsteps of their cherished friend whom the Lord has called home.

They tender their sympathy, first, to the bereaved widow, and, second, to all friends, and rejoice with them that the memories of his pure life are so redolent with all that is sacred and lovely.

F. LEE FORMAN,
N. B. COY,
Denver, Col., Feb. 6, 1886.   HELEN DILL.

QUINCY SCHOOL ASSOCIATION.

At the meeting of the Executive Committee of the Quincy School Association of Boston, held Feb. 12, the following testimonial to the late Dr. John D. Philbrick was unanimously adopted, and it was voted that a copy be sent to the family of the deceased : —

We, the officers and members of the Quincy School Association of Boston, desirous of expressing our heart-felt sorrow at the death of the late Dr. John D. Philbrick, the first master of our school, lovingly place upon the records of the Association this expression of our esteem and affection for our former teacher and early friend.

We deeply feel the loss which not only this Association, but the cause of education in general, has sustained in being deprived of the zeal, energy, and wisdom which characterized his administration of the various offices which he was called upon to fill, and for which he was so eminently qualified.

We personally lament the loss to this Association of one of its chief officers, whose hearty interest in its formation was an earnest manifestation of his affection for his former pupils in the school organized and made practically successful by his personal exertions and enthusiasm.

We bear our testimony to his abounding kindness and amiability amid the vexations of the schoolroom, and to the unconcealed affection which he bore for all with whom he was associated.

We tender to the widow and relatives our sincere sympathy in their bereavement. Sorrowing at the departure of husband and friend, they are yet blessed in the memory of his worth and the fact that thousands mourn with them, and bear unanimous testimony to his superior qualities of mind and heart.

SPENCER W. RICHARDSON, *Prest.* ⎫
B. W. PUTNAM, *First Vice-Prest.* ⎪ *Quincy*
F. W. BULLARD, *Treas.* ⎬ *School*
Ç. H. BRIGHAM, *Sec.* ⎭ *Association.*

TRUSTEES OF BATES COLLEGE.

Dear Mrs. Philbrick : —

The following is a copy of the resolutions passed by the Trustees of Bates College in reference to the death of your late husband : —

· *Resolved*, That we recognize in the death of Hon. John D. Philbrick, LL.D., for many years an honored member of our Board, the departure of one of the most helpful and zealous friends of this college, whose valuable services and hopeful spirit, remembered with gratitude, remain as an inspiration to our work ; a gentleman of genial and catholic mind, whose services, of inestimable value to the educational interests of the nation, fitly received the highest national recognition.

Resolved, That a copy of these resolutions be forwarded to Mrs. Philbrick, to whom we tender our sincerest sympathy.

O. B. CHENEY, Prest.
L. G. JORDAN, Sec.

Lewiston, Maine, July 12, 1886.

TOWN OF DEERFIELD.

DEERFIELD, N. H., March, 1886.

The Resolutions herewith enclosed represent the action taken by the people of Deerfield on the death of Hon. John D. Philbrick.

Very respectfully,
G. B. HOITT, Town Clerk.

The citizens of the town of Deerfield, having learned with regret of the death of Hon. John D. Philbrick, would place on their records and transmit to his family, a testimonial of his worth, and an expression of their sense of loss in his decease. They recognize the service he has rendered to the cause of education, and would witness to its great value. They also gratefully acknowledge their indebtedness to him, for his interest in his native town, especially for his wise and careful selection of the books for the library, with which his name is associated. Its value is in no small degree owing to his painstaking labor.

They would testify to his worth as a man, and to the great good that his life-work has accomplished.

Press of
Berwick & Smith,
Boston.

www.ingramcontent.com/pod-product-compliance
Lightning Source LLC
Chambersburg PA
CBHW020117030726

47498CB00006B/2141